THE WHISPERING WINDMILL

THE MYSTERY HOUSE SERIES, BOOK FIFTEEN

Eva Pohler

Eva Pohler Books
20011 Park Ranch
San Antonio, Texas 78259
www.evapohler.com

Publisher's Note: This is a work of fiction. Names, characters, places, and incidents are a product of the author's imagination. Locales and public names are sometimes used for atmospheric purposes. Any resemblance to actual people, living or dead, or to businesses, companies, events, institutions, or locales is completely coincidental.

Edited by Alexis Rigoni

Book Cover Design by B Rose DesignZ

The Whispering Windmill/ Eva Pohler. -- 1st ed.
ISBN: 978-1-958390-83-2

Contents

In memory of Thomas Alva Edison and Henry Ford, benefactors to the modern world.

CHAPTER ONE

Sue's Confession

"Sue?" Ellen cried when she answered the door. "Oh, my gosh, what happened to you?"

Tanya, who stood six-feet tall beside Ellen's five-foot-ten, widened her eyes at the short brunette standing in the doorway. "You look amazing!"

"She's half the woman she was the last time we saw her," Ellen pointed out.

"Are you going to ask me in? Or am I supposed to stand out here all evening?"

"Oh, sorry!" Ellen made way for her friend as she added, "We're just in shock. You never said anything."

As Sue, who stood at barely five feet tall, entered, Moseby, Ellen's little black dog, greeted her, running in between her legs before following her to Ellen's living room. "I've lost seventy-five pounds, but a lot of people haven't even noticed."

"Blind people?" Tanya wanted to know. "Because it's pretty darn obvious."

"You just haven't seen me in a while." Sue made her way to an armchair beside Ellen's fireplace. "I need to sit down. Tom and I just had the fight of our lives."

"What?" Ellen followed her friends to her living room, where she and Tanya took a seat. Moseby jumped into her lap. "What happened? Well, first, do you need anything to drink?"

"I had a Cherry Coke in the car, I'm fine."

"Sue, what happened with Tom?" Tanya asked gently as she nervously twirled a strand of her blonde hair with a finger.

Ellen blinked a few times, still adjusting to her friend's new appearance. She couldn't recall Sue ever being this thin. She was almost the same size as Ellen now—or within thirty pounds. Ellen thought she could stand to lose seventy-five pounds herself.

"As you know, we spent Christmas at our house in Montana on the reservation," Sue began. "And, well, I decided to stay on my own over the past few months. I just got back yesterday."

Ellen and Tanya exchanged looks of confusion.

Tanya leaned forward. "Why did you keep it a secret from us? We've asked you out for lunch a dozen times, and you've always had some excuse."

"I didn't lie exactly. I was busy."

"Doing what?" Ellen wanted to know.

Sue brushed her brown bangs from her eyes and glanced around. "Where's Brian?"

"He's taking a shower in the back of the house," Ellen replied, a knot forming in her gut. "What's going on, Sue?"

"I've been having the time of my life! I gambled at the Blackfeet Casino all day, came home to a clean house and a delicious meal made by a woman I found up there—Angelina. She cooked, cleaned, and gave me facials and massages. It was hard to come home, honestly."

"Talk about living like a queen," Ellen murmured.

"But you've always hated gambling," Tanya pointed out.

Ellen nodded. "We tried to get you to stay longer in Vegas while we were working on the Hoover Dam mystery, and you refused."

"I know," Sue admitted. "But I like it now. I more than like it."

Tanya shifted in her seat. "That's why you and Tom are fighting. How much money have you lost?"

Sue bit her bottom lip. "Keep in mind that I've lost weight and have had a blast doing it."

Ellen leaned forward. "Sue? How much money have you lost?"

"Thirty grand," Sue confessed.

"What?" Ellen and Tanya cried together.

I just can't get enough. I'm especially fond of one machine called the 'Mo Mummy.'"

"You've been playing the slots?" Ellen scratched her head, unable to believe this wasn't a joke.

Sue climbed to her feet and put her hands on her hips, in warrior-ready fashion. "It's not as bad as everyone seems to think. I had fun for three months—three solid months. I won some big money, and I lost some, too, but it was exciting. Thrilling. Like meeting a new lover, you know? That level of thrilling. I made it to VIP status, which means I ran over $400,000 dollars through their machines, and of that, I only lost thirty."

"Only?" Tanya repeated.

"I earned free stays at the casino, expensive steak dinners, free spa treatments, and all kinds of perks. I could drink free Cherry Cokes all day long. And I lost seventy-five pounds! How much money have I spent on special diets, the lap band, therapy, Jenny Craig, you name it? Who knew that I could lose weight and have a blast doing it? I got on Zepbound, that new weight loss medication, and one meal a day is enough for me these days, especially when I'm playing the slots!"

"But thirty grand?" Tanya said again.

"People spend that on vacations each year," Sue argued. "I work hard helping others move on and find peace. Why can't I spend some money on myself to have fun? What's the point of striking oil and finding gold if we can't enjoy it?"

"What does Tom say?" Ellen asked.

Sue returned to her seat. "He wants to sell the Montana house, to remove the temptation."

Ellen would hate to see the property go. She had great memories of the place—not only of solving the mystery of the ghost of Blackfeet Nation, but of trips there with her friends and family.

"Is that what you'll do?" Tanya asked with a frown. "Sell it?"

"I told Tom it would be over my dead body, and that's where we are. I think he's plotting the easiest way to do me in."

"Oh, Sue." Ellen rolled her eyes.

"Maybe our trip to Michigan will give you some perspective," Tanya put in. "Get your mind off things for a while."

"I hope you're right," Sue admitted. "When I'm not playing the machine, I'm watching other people play it on YouTube. There's even an app on my phone. I told Tom I'd delete it, but I haven't yet. It's all I think about. Even now, I'd rather be there."

Ellen and Tanya exchanged frowns.

"We leave in the morning for Detroit," Ellen reminded her, holding up the itinerary she wanted to go over. "Have you packed yet?"

"I haven't *un*packed," Sue said. "Angelina washed my clothes before I left, thank goodness, so I just have a few things to change out."

"Don't you think you should get started, then?" Tanya suggested. "We fly out at ten o'clock. And you better not bail on us."

Sue climbed to her feet again. "I'm not going to bail on you. When I have I ever?"

"When have you ever been addicted to a slot machine?" Ellen argued.

"Good point," Sue conceded as she made her way to the front door. "But I'm not going to bail."

"I hope not, because John Coleman's phone call sounded desperate," Ellen added. "Something's going on at that windmill in Greenfield Village. It might be another haunting."

"We're depending on your help," Tanya reminded her.

"I'm not going to bail!" Sue said again. "I'll see you guys in the morning."

Ellen handed over the itinerary. "Look this over and call me if you want me to change anything."

"Aye, aye, Captain."

Once Sue had left, Tanya turned to Ellen. "I can't believe it. Thirty grand?"

"Maybe she just needs some distance between her and the casino," Ellen said.

"I hope you're right. If she does bail on us, I'll never forgive her."

Ellen switched off the bathroom light and padded into the bedroom, toweling off the last bit of moisturizer from her hands. Moseby, their long-haired miniature Dachshund and poodle mix, was already curled up dead-center in the bed like a spoiled prince, snoring softly. Brian was pulling back the covers on his side when he looked up and grinned.

"Think he'll move if we ask nicely?"

Ellen laughed and fluffed her pillow. "Doubtful. He's already claimed the territory."

She sat on the edge of the bed and leaned down to scratch Moseby's floppy ears. "I wish I could take him with me," she said softly. "But it's going to be cold in Michigan, and we'll be tromping around Greenfield Village most of the time. I don't think he'd appreciate the snow or the ghosts."

Brian climbed in beside her and patted Moseby's back. "He'll be fine. We'll have long talks about squirrels and the state of the backyard. I might even let him watch a movie with me—something manly, with explosions."

Ellen smiled, but it didn't quite reach her eyes.

Brian shifted to face her. "Is it just Moseby you're worried about? Or is there something else?"

She hesitated, tugging the edge of the quilt over her lap. "It's Sue."

His brow furrowed.

"She spent three months at her place on the Blackfeet reservation," Ellen said quietly. "So she could go to the casino every day. Every day, Brian. She lost thirty grand on a slot machine. Can you believe it?"

Brian let out a low whistle.

"She and Tom are fighting, as you can imagine. And she looked so preoccupied tonight when we were talking about the trip. It's like she's not even excited about going."

Brian reached over and took her hand. "That's rough. But she's not doing this alone. She's got you and Tanya. And this trip—it might be exactly what she needs. A change of scenery. A reason to focus on something bigger than herself. She's tough, El. She'll bounce back."

Ellen swallowed, grateful for his steady optimism. "I hope you're right."

"I usually am," he said with a wink. "And she's got you. You always see people, even when they're trying their best not to be seen."

Ellen looked over at him, her eyes soft. "You know, I don't say it enough—but I'm really grateful for you. For your steadiness. Your heart. The way you make everything feel . . . less overwhelming."

Brian smiled and brushed a strand of hair from her cheek. "I'm the lucky one. All those souls you've helped—living and dead—I'm proud of you. Just don't forget to take care of yourself too, okay?"

She leaned in and kissed him. "I'll miss you."

"I'll be right here when you get back," he said.

They settled into bed, Moseby nestled between them like a furry little baby, and as the room dimmed into stillness, Ellen let herself believe that maybe everything would turn out all right.

CHAPTER TWO

Dearborn Inn

The Uber driver's tires crunched over the icy, brick-paved driveway as he pulled up to the front of the Dearborn Inn.

Ellen pressed her face to the frosty window, leaning in for a better look. "Oh, would you look at that," she said, her breath fogging up the glass. "Isn't it beautiful?"

"I feel like we just rolled into a snow globe," Sue murmured from beside her in the back seat, hugging her coat around her shoulders.

Tanya leaned forward in the front passenger's seat. "This is not your average hotel."

The inn stood proud and stately, its red brick façade perfectly symmetrical, lined with white-trimmed windows and capped with a steep, slate roof dusted in fresh snow. Tall chimneys stretched into the pale gray sky, and a grand columned portico framed the front entrance. Despite the cold, small evergreen shrubs dotted the path to the door, their branches heavy with frost.

"How long will you ladies be in town?" their Uber driver, a big man with long, wavy, black hair and small, metal-rimmed spectacles, asked. He appeared to be in his early fifties.

"That's yet to be determined," Sue answered from the back seat as she rummaged through her wallet for a cash tip. "It depends on how long it takes us to solve a mystery."

"Oh?" the driver asked with raised brows. "What mystery?"

The three friends quickly recapped why they were there.

The Uber driver handed Tanya his card. "If you ladies need any help, please call. I used to be the liaison between the Basilica of Sainte Anne and the city of Detroit, and I know a lot of its history. I would be happy to show you around and share what I know, free of charge."

"Really?" Tanya took his card. "Thanks, C.W. We'll call if we need you."

Ellen stepped out into the brisk Michigan air and shivered as a gust of wind barreled through her coat. She moved toward the trunk, where the driver caught up to unload their luggage.

"This place was built in 1931," C.W. pointed out. "Commissioned by Henry Ford to house airport travelers and visitors to Greenfield Village. Designed by Albert Kahn."

"You do know a lot, don't you?" Ellen said, as she took her suitcase from him.

"I'm happy to help in any way I can," the driver assured them. "If you're researching ghosts in Detroit, there are some places that you must visit—Michigan Grand Central, the Basilica of Sainte Anne, the Eloise—that's not far from here. Oh, and the Whitney. All these places must certainly contain ghosts."

"Thank you, C.W." Sue handed him a generous tip. "We'll text you if we need you."

"Don't hesitate. I'm intrigued by your mystery."

Together, the three women trudged through the slush toward the grand entrance. The double doors opened with a hiss, welcoming them into a warm, lavish lobby. A wave of polished wood, antique furniture, and the faint scent of old books wrapped around Ellen like a blanket.

The space was magnificent—high ceilings adorned with ornate plaster molding, plush area rugs in deep burgundy and navy, and crystal chandeliers that dripped light like icicles. Wingback chairs and tufted sofas were arranged into intimate groupings, encouraging conversation as a classical piano piece played quietly from hidden speakers.

A tall, thin man in a navy wool coat stood up from one of the couches near the fireplace. Appearing to be in his mid-forties, he approached them with cautious urgency, his dark-rimmed glasses slightly fogged. He held a gray fedora in his hands, which Ellen supposed he needed to keep his nearly bald head warm.

"You must be the Ghost Healers," he said, extending his hand with relief. "John Coleman. We spoke on the phone."

Ellen shook his hand first. "Ellen. This is Tanya, and that's Sue."

"I can't tell you how grateful I am that you're here," John said. "Honestly, you're our last hope."

"I get told that a lot," Sue teased with her usual charm.

John chuckled. "Let's have a seat. I'll fill you in."

They followed him to the sitting area near the hearth, where heat from the fire licked at their legs as they settled into deep, soft couches. Ellen took in the carved walnut coffee table and the delicate, blue china vases, the kind of refinement she associated more with a historic mansion than a hotel lobby.

"So, how was the flight?" John asked, attempting pleasantries. "Not too turbulent?"

"It wasn't too bad," Tanya said.

"But this weather is another story," Ellen added. "We left San Antonio in the eighties—already flip-flop season. This," she gestured toward the icy windows, "feels like we landed on a different planet."

"That's Michigan in March," John said. "Could be sunny tomorrow or a blizzard. It likes to keep us guessing."

Sue pulled her jacket more tightly around her. "It's a good thing I packed my Montana clothes."

John leaned forward, resting his elbows on his knees. "We normally reopen Greenfield Village in April, just after Easter. We close every winter for maintenance, safety reasons, weather. But this year . . ." He hesitated, pressing his lips together. "There's serious talk about delaying the opening. Possibly canceling the entire spring season."

Ellen sat straighter. "Because of the windmill?"

"Yes." He glanced around, lowering his voice. "Like I said on the phone, we've had an increase in visitor complaints. Whispering voices near the Farris Windmill—disembodied, eerie. Some people thought it was a prank, others thought it was a speaker malfunction. But we checked. There's no audio equipment out there."

"What kind of voices?" Tanya asked.

"Faint at first," John said. "But they've gotten stronger. One woman swore someone whispered her name. A group of schoolkids heard what sounded like a man reciting numbers—over and over. A retired couple got so spooked they demanded a refund and left halfway through the tour. And they weren't the only visitors wanting their money back."

"And this only happens at the windmill?" Ellen asked, eyes sharp.

"Mostly, yes. Though a few docents say they've heard things near the Menlo Lab, too. But nothing consistent. The windmill is the epicenter."

Sue leaned forward. "Any crimes or murders associated with the place?"

John frowned. "The Farris Windmill is the oldest windmill in the country. Built around 1633, moved here from Cape Cod in the late 1930s. But I'm afraid I don't know much beyond that."

"We'll start there," Ellen said. "We've got some research to do."

"I knew I called the right people," John said with a grateful smile.

Sue rubbed her eyes. "I'm sorry—but I've been up since five, and my brain's not quite firing on all cylinders."

"Like it ever does," Ellen teased.

"That's true, Ellen," Sue said with a grin. "It's a good thing I don't need as many cylinders as most people."

Chuckling, John stood, brushing invisible lint from his coat. "Then you'll be pleased to know I've made special arrangements."

"Oh?" Tanya asked.

"I've booked the Patrick Henry House for you. It's the largest of six colonial homes next to the inn. Completely restored, beautifully furnished, and all yours for as long as you need."

Sue's eyes lit up. "Now that's more like it."

John chuckled again. "Follow me, and I'll help you get settled in."

As the women gathered their bags and followed him back into the cold, Ellen felt a surge of excitement shoot through her bones. There was nothing like the start of a new mystery.

"Lead the way," Ellen said to John with a grin.

CHAPTER THREE

The Patrick Henry House

By the time John Coleman guided them through a white iron gate and down a winding brick path toward the Patrick Henry House, the last blush of sunset had faded into a moody lavender sky. The colonial mansion stood regal in the growing dusk, its symmetrical façade bathed in the warm glow of outdoor lanterns. Snow clung to the shrubs that lined the walk, and frost crept like lace along the bottom panes of the tall windows.

"Oh, my stars," Sue whispered as they stepped onto the wide front porch. "We are not in Texas anymore."

Ellen smiled, already admiring the architecture—white clapboard siding, black shutters, a steep-pitched roof. The stately house had the soul of a museum and the warmth of a home. It was easy to imagine it lit by candlelight, with powdered wigs and Revolutionary talk echoing through the halls.

John unlocked the door with a skeleton key and pushed it open with a dramatic flourish as he removed his gray fedora from his head. "Welcome to your home away from home."

The scent of old wood, lemon polish, and just a hint of firewood greeted them. Ellen stepped inside first, struck immediately by the elegance of the wide center hall, with gleaming hardwood floors and a grand staircase curving gently up to the second level. Crown molding framed every doorway, and antique sconces cast a golden glow on the cream walls.

"Oh, I'm going to love this," Tanya breathed as she walked into the front sitting room. "It's like staying in a living piece of history."

"You could film a period drama in here," Ellen agreed, running her fingers along the polished surface of a Queen Anne sideboard.

They toured the main floor first, oohing and ahhing through the richly furnished sitting room with its fireplace and velvet drapes, then on to a formal dining room with a ten-foot-long table and gleaming silver tea service. Every detail felt curated, from the oil portraits lining the walls to the brass candlesticks and spindle-back chairs.

When they reached the large, white kitchen in the back of the main wing—updated but still charmingly colonial—Tanya said, "I call dibs on not cooking."

"Same," Sue replied. "This is a vacation-slash-investigation. I vote we order in and keep the oven purely decorative."

"Too bad Angelina couldn't come with us," Ellen teased.

"It really is," Sue agreed. "I asked her if she'd come live with me in San Antonio and continue what she was doing in Montana. I even said she could have my husband, but I guess it wasn't enough to tempt her."

John shook his head and showed them the layout of the house, explaining that the east and west wings couldn't be accessed from the central hall. "They're beautiful but a bit isolated," he said. "You'd have to go outside to reach them—no interior doors connect them to the main structure."

"Well, that's a no from me," Sue said immediately. "No way am I walking through the snow in my pajamas to make a circle of protection with my friends."

That brought them to the main floor's master bedroom—a spacious room with an intricately carved four-poster bed, a private bath, and tall windows draped in brocade.

"Now this," Sue said, spinning slowly in the center of the rug, "is where I shall rest my weary bones."

Tanya raised an eyebrow. "Already staked your claim?"

Sue glanced toward the grand staircase just outside the bedroom. "You know me and stairs. This ankle's been clicking since the plane landed."

Ellen and Tanya exchanged a look. They always gave Sue the downstairs room, and Ellen couldn't exactly argue with the logic. But her knees had been giving her a hard time lately, and the idea of climbing stairs after a long day of ghost hunting didn't thrill her either.

"The other downstairs bedroom is also nice," John said, leading them to a smaller room near the back of the house off the kitchen. It was charming enough, with a spindle bed, floral wallpaper, and a handstitched quilt. "But it doesn't have an attached bath. You'd have to walk through the sitting room to use the powder room."

Tanya grimaced. "So, basically I'd have to sneak past Sue like a burglar if I had to pee at two in the morning."

Sue grinned. "I do sleep with one eye open."

Ellen chuckled but stepped toward the staircase. "Let's see what's upstairs before we declare war over bathroom proximity."

The staircase creaked beneath their boots as she followed Tanya up, and Ellen tried not to picture it creaking for entirely different reasons in the dead of night. At the top, a wide landing opened into a cor-ridor flanked by doors on either side. The ceilings sloped gently with the roofline, and the scent up here was more attic than polish—cozy and nostalgic.

Each new bedroom was more charming than the last. One had deep blue wallpaper with a canopy bed and a writing desk by the win-dow. Another was done in sage green and white, with a chaise lounge and delicate floral curtains. Every single one had its own *en suite* bath-room, complete with clawfoot tubs and vintage fixtures.

"Well," Tanya said, hands on her hips. "Looks like I found my room."

Ellen nodded toward the blue room. "That one's calling to me."

"I knew you'd find something you liked up there," Sue said from the bottom of the stairs.

"You're lucky we're easy to please," Tanya called down.

They gathered back downstairs, where John handed them each an old-fashioned brass key.

"Again, thank you for coming," he said. "Take the evening to settle in. I've left some brochures and maps in the kitchen, along with some sample reports from our security team and maintenance staff. We've documented some of the more unusual incidents around the windmill."

"We'll dive into it first thing tomorrow," Ellen said.

John nodded. "I'll pick you up in the morning. Ten o'clock okay? I thought we'd start with a tour of Greenfield Village."

"Can we make it ten fifteen?" Sue asked.

"Ten-fifteen it is," he replied as he returned his hat to his head. "Goodnight, ladies. If you need anything, my cell is written on the kitchen bulletin board."

Once the front door clicked shut behind him, Sue let out a long sigh. "He seems nice. Nervous, but nice."

"They're probably all a little spooked," Ellen said. "I would be, too, if I ran a hundred-year-old history park and it suddenly started whispering to tourists."

"Yeah." Tanya grabbed her luggage from beside the front door. "This isn't your run-of-the-mill haunting."

Ellen turned to Sue. "Why did you ask for an additional fifteen minutes?"

Sue blushed. "I know you won't understand this, but I need at least that much time on YouTube with the Mo Mummy machine when I first wake up, especially now, when I can't play on it in person."

Tanya groaned. "You've got a serious problem, Sue."

"Everyone has problems, Tanya, and mine's not hurting any-one—not yet, at least."

Tanya arched a brow but said nothing as she turned and headed up the stairs with her luggage.

Ellen lingered in the sitting room, gazing out the window at the snowy path. A breeze stirred the trees beyond the fence, bare limbs rat-tling like bones. In the distance, a soft whir of wind danced through the branches—almost like a whisper.

Ellen tugged the covers up around her lap, propped a pillow behind her back, and adjusted the reading glasses perched on her nose. The bed-room's antique furnishings glowed softly in the amber light of the brass bedside lamp, gently illuminating the floral wallpaper. Outside the tall windows, a March wind rattled the panes, but inside, the Patrick Henry House was warm, still, and peaceful—at least for the moment.

She'd just spoken to Brian on the phone for a quick check-in and was missing him and Moseby when she reached for the manila folder John Coleman had left for them on the kitchen counter. Ellen had slipped the folder under her arm along with her favorite tea and retreated upstairs after Sue declared it was "officially pajama o'clock."

Now, she began flipping through the contents. Typed notes, photocopied emails, and handwritten witness statements—some recent, others dating back a few months. She skimmed the headers: *Windmill Whispers Intensify, Unexplained Machinery Noise, Child Claims to See "Man in the Blades."*

She paused at a witness report from last September.

Date: September 1

Visitor Name: Cynthia Mallory

Incident: "Around 3:00 p.m., while standing near the windmill with my two grandsons, we heard what sounded like a woman humming. It was faint but close, as if it came from the blades themselves. When I looked up, one of the boys asked, 'Who's the lady standing in the top window?' There was no one there. But we all saw movement. I don't scare easily, but we left after that."

Ellen's skin prickled. She imagined the silhouette of a woman behind the small window of the mill tower, peering down at tourists. It reminded her of the lady of the lighthouse in Biloxi. She turned the page.

Date September 25

Visitor Name: James Rodriguez

Incident: "My wife and son and I were visiting the Farris Windmill when I saw a shadow of a man wearing a black hat in the tower window. When I pointed him out to my wife and son, he vanished. I know I didn't imagine it."

More reports, from October.

Date: October 8

Visitor Name: Fred Amari

Incident: "My ten-year-old daughter and I were admiring the Farris Windmill this morning when we heard what sounded like a child's voice cry, 'Help me!' We looked all around the windmill and in the nearby buildings but never found the source of the cry. We returned to the windmill and heard it again, but this time, with a threat: 'Help me, or you'll be sorry!' I told my daughter that enough is enough, and we left the park and asked for our money back."

Date: October 12

Staff Member Name: Betty Nelson

Incident: "While dusting the shelves in Menlo Lab on the second floor, I saw a shadow man wearing a black hat standing at the top of the stairs. He tipped his hat at me and disappeared down the stairs. I should have followed him, but I couldn't move for many minutes. I've never seen anything like it before."

That was two sightings of a hat man, Ellen thought. Turning the page over, she read a report from early November.

Date: November 2

Visitor Name: Deanna Humphreys

Incident: "It was just before noon when my husband and I walked over to the windmill. The blades were barely moving. At first, I thought the murmuring was caused by the movement of the blades. But the closer we got to the windmill the clearer the whispering became. Someone was reciting numbers. My husband opened the door to the tower, and we both peered in. There was no one inside. But we both felt a strange chill inside—even colder than the air on the outside. We didn't want a refund but thought someone should know."

Ellen yawned, determined to read one more report.

Date: February 21

Staff Member Name: Darrell Hines

Incident: "During scheduled maintenance, I was inspecting the mill's upper gears when the air turned *icy*. It was a clear, mild day. No reason for the temp to drop like that. I heard a whisper behind me, like a woman's voice, right in my ear: 'Help me.' I looked around, no one. Got out of there fast."

Ellen swallowed. She could practically feel the breath at her own ear, the soft words hanging in the air like smoke. She set the folder aside and glanced around her room—still safe, still silent. But the unease lingered.

She flipped to a final report—a hand-scrawled note, no date.

"The voices only come when the blades spin. And sometimes they spin even when the wind doesn't blow."

Ellen stared at the words. The windmill was old, mechanical. It shouldn't move without wind.

As she was about to close the folder, a sticky Post-it note dropped into her lap. On it was a note from John: "Not everyone at Henry Ford is on board with your investigation, so please only report your activities and findings to me."

She reread the note, wondering if there would be anyone causing her and her team any problems.

She closed the folder and laid it on the other side of the bed, where Brian would be lying if he were there with her.

Then, from somewhere downstairs, a faint creak. Just the house settling, she told herself.

Still, she decided to leave her lamp on for the night.

Just in case.

CHAPTER FOUR

Greenfield Village

Ellen tugged her crocheted beanie down over her ears as the unmistakable *chuff-chuff-chuff* of an approaching engine turned her gaze to the road outside the Patrick Henry House. A black Model T Ford rolled into view, its paint glistening despite the overcast March sky. With its brass accents and high carriage wheels, it looked like something straight out of an old newsreel.

"Well, would you look at that," Tanya said, setting down her mug of coffee and hurrying to the door with Sue and Ellen behind her.

John Coleman grinned from behind the large steering wheel, gloved hands steady. He tipped his gray fedora as he said, "Your chariot awaits, ladies."

"Dibs on the front seat!" Tanya called, already making her way down the front steps.

Sue blinked at the vehicle and arched a skeptical brow. "That thing has brakes, right? And I don't mean *Flintstones* brakes."

John chuckled. "It's got brakes, shock absorbers, and exactly twenty horsepower of sheer adrenaline. You'll be perfectly safe. And possibly cold."

"Great," Sue muttered, pulling her coat tighter. "Just what I've always wanted: a bumpy ride in a glorified tractor."

Ellen laughed, sliding into the back beside her. The seat was firm but surprisingly comfortable. "C'mon, Sue. This is history on wheels. Where's your sense of adventure?"

"I left it in my suitcase with the thermal socks I *should've* worn," she grumbled as the Model T jolted to life again.

As they rumbled down the quiet street toward Greenfield Village, the wind carried the sharp bite of early Michigan spring. The sky above was a pewter dome, the trees along the sidewalk skeletal against the gray.

"So," John called over his shoulder, "how did you all sleep?"

"No ghostly visitors," Ellen said. "At least, not yet."

Sue rolled her eyes. "Speak for yourself. I swear I heard something thumping upstairs around midnight."

"That was probably Tanya doing yoga in her room," Ellen teased.

Tanya glanced back with a grin. "It's called stretching, thank you very much. My joints don't like stairs either."

Ellen noticed large birds that seemed to be grazing in the grass on the roadside. They were beautiful and elegant, like swans, but had the color of geese.

"Are those geese?" she asked John.

"Canadian geese. They're a nuisance, really."

She saw more along the roadside. "So lovely."

"Not the piles of poop they leave behind," John remarked.

"I say the same thing about Tom," Sue said with a grin.

John smiled but didn't comment. He turned the Model T through the main entrance of Greenfield Village, where the iconic arched gate loomed over the drive. The gate was closed to the public, but a staff member bundled in a thick jacket and knit cap stepped forward to unlock it and wave them through.

Inside, the village was empty, save for a few employees shoveling snow from walkways or performing quiet maintenance on the historic buildings. The absence of tourists made the entire place seem surreal, as though they were stepping into a carefully preserved world just for them.

Their first stop was a modest white farmhouse nestled behind a white picket fence.

"Here we are," John said, parking in front of Henry Ford's childhood home. "This house is exactly how it was on the day Henry's mother died. He insisted it be preserved that way."

Ellen climbed out, pulling her coat tighter as the cold nipped at her cheeks. "That's a little morbid, don't you think?"

John folded his arms. "He said that if his mother were to return from the grave, he wanted her to recognize the place and feel comfortable in it."

"I think it's sweet," Tanya put in.

They stepped through the creaky front door and into the simple, timeworn interior. A narrow hallway led to a cozy parlor filled with period furnishings. A rocking chair sat near the window, a crocheted afghan draped over its back as if someone had only just risen from it. A fire sat unlit in the hearth, the ashes swept clean.

Ellen had moved toward the sitting room, admiring the lace curtains and wallpaper, when a sudden chill traced its fingers along her spine.

She paused.

Something shifted in the air—an absence of warmth, like stepping into a forgotten root cellar. Goosebumps rose along her arms.

She turned to see Tanya standing stock-still beside the fireplace.

Tanya's brow furrowed. "Do you feel that?"

"Yeah," Ellen murmured.

Sue stepped forward, rubbing her arms. "Either this place has poor insulation, or we've got company."

John blinked, looking around. "Is it cold in here? I didn't notice anything."

Tanya looked at Ellen. "Looks like we've got our work cut out for us."

"Should we try to make contact?" Ellen asked quietly.

Sue shook her head. "Let's finish the tour and decide where to start. I'd rather get the full picture before poking the hornet's nest."

John nodded, visibly relieved, and led them back outside.

The Model T tour resumed, taking them next to the Wright brothers' home and bicycle shop, where John shared stories of Orville and Wilbur tinkering through endless nights. Then on to the red-brick Logan County Courthouse where Abraham Lincoln once practiced law, and then to the Firestone farmhouse, where Harvey Firestone spent his childhood.

"Harvey Firestone and Thomas Edison used to go camping with Henry Ford," John told them. "They were great friends for many years. Ford and Firestone funded a lot of Edison's research and inventing. They both worshipped Edison, and the three of them together made the media go nuts. They never could go anywhere without a mob following them, taking photos, and asking for speeches. Edison never would give a speech, but Ford would."

Ellen soaked it all in—the creak of porch boards, the smell of aged wood, the way each building held the hum of forgotten lives. But with every stop, she also noticed flickers. A shadow in a window. A creak where no foot had fallen. Cold spots that moved rather than lingered.

"There's a story they always tell," John continued. "It's probably an urban legend. They say one time their car broke down near a farm, and the farmer, not knowing who the men were, came to help. He said the tires might be bad, and Firestone said, 'No, it's not the tires. I'm Harvey Firestone, and those tires are in good condition.' 'Could be the battery,' the farmer said. Edison said, 'No, I'm Thomas Edison, the inventor of that battery, and I know it's not the problem.' 'Let's open the hood,' the farmer suggested. 'Could be the engine.' 'It's not the engine,' Ford said. 'I'm Henry Ford, and I made that engine.'"

The ladies laughed.

And then they arrived at the Farris Windmill.

It rose high above them, a towering structure of weathered gray beams and whirling blades that creaked gently in the wind. A dusting of snow clung to its stone base, and the windmill's door sat slightly ajar.

"This is where the whispering has been most frequent," John said, stepping out of the car. "Visitors have reported hearing voices in multiple languages—English, Dutch, even something that sounded like French. Maintenance workers say they've heard it at all hours, especially around dusk."

The wind rustled through the bare trees as Ellen approached the windmill's door. Something about the structure drew her in. It felt alive—listening, maybe even watching.

John went on, "This is the oldest windmill in the U.S., built in the 1630s in Cape Cod and brought here piece by piece. Some think it's the wood, that maybe it carries memories. Others think it's the location."

"Any reported deaths?" Sue asked. "Murders, crimes, people ground up in the gears?"

John blinked. "None that I know of. But that doesn't mean there isn't a story buried in the wood."

Tanya circled the structure, craning her neck to look up at the blades. "You know, for all its charm, this place gives me the creeps."

"There's something wrong about it," Ellen said softly. She pressed her hand to the wooden frame of the door, half expecting a jolt. None came. But something flickered in the periphery of her mind. A whisper—too faint to understand.

Sue sighed. "Okay, I vote we start here. You said that this is the epicenter, right?"

John nodded. "It's definitely the most active spot."

"I'm hungry," Tanya said. "Why don't we regroup after lunch?"

"Sounds good to me," Ellen agreed.

They climbed back into the Model T, subdued now, the weight of the place settling in. As John drove them slowly through the village, past lanterns and chimneys and houses frozen in time, Ellen couldn't help but feel they were being watched by more than just security cameras.

History wasn't sleeping here.

It was whispering.

And it wanted to be heard.

CHAPTER FIVE

The Whispering Windmill

The three women huddled around a polished wood table in the corner of *Lamy's Diner*, a 1940s-themed eatery situated smack in the middle of the indoor part of the Henry Ford Museum, which was open to the public and bustling with patrons. The chrome and Formica glimmered under pendant lights, where the three friends leaned over their steaming bowls of tomato soup and chicken salad sandwiches.

After giving them badges for free entry, John Coleman had dropped them off fifteen minutes earlier and promised to return later in the afternoon.

"Well," Sue said, unwrapping her silverware, "so far no one's tried to possess me or pull my hair, so that's a win."

"Give it time," Ellen teased. "There's a group of school children about to come out of the giant-screen movie theater."

Tanya took a sip of her tea, eyeing the other diners, before pulling out her phone. "Let's make good use of this downtime. The Farris Windmill has to have some kind of paper trail."

Ellen nodded, retrieving her own phone and typing the name into her browser. "F-A-R-R-I-S Windmill . . . Cape Cod . . . Oh wow. This thing really does go back to the seventeenth century."

"1633," Tanya confirmed, reading aloud. "Built in West Harwich, Massachusetts. It's the oldest surviving windmill in the U.S. Moved a bunch of times over the centuries before being donated to the museum."

Ellen scrolled through an archived article from a local Massachusetts paper. Her eyes paused on a passage that made her breath hitch. "Here's something . . . It says the windmill was briefly closed in the early 1800s after a shipwreck."

"Wait, what?" Sue looked up in mid-bite. "A windmill caused a shipwreck?"

"That's what this article suggests." Ellen tapped her screen and turned it for them to see. "'A deadly navigation error was blamed on the inaccurate orientation of the mill's vanes, which, according to the captain of the *Sea Wren*, appeared from the shoreline to signal safe passage through a hazardous reef. The vessel ran aground during a storm. Most of the crew perished.'"

"Dang," Tanya whispered.

"There's more," Ellen added. "After the wreck, the town held an inquest. They blamed the miller—an Alfred Wilkes—for failing to maintain proper vane positioning. But Alfred died shortly after. Found crushed beneath one of the arms during repairs."

Sue frowned. "Sounds fishy."

"Definitely," Ellen murmured, rereading the line. "Unsolved, even by 1800s standards."

"So, we've got a fatal shipwreck, a possibly sabotaged windmill, and a dead miller," Tanya said, pulling out her tiny leather notebook. "That's a start."

Ellen leaned back in her chair, her soup forgotten. The chill from Henry Ford's home still lingered in her bones, and now this—tragedy layered beneath charming shingles and old wood.

"We need to go back," she said.

Sue sighed and pushed her tray away. "I agree—though I was just starting to digest."

Tanya was already standing, brushing breadcrumbs from her lap. "Let's go. I've got enough curiosity now to fuel me through a blizzard."

They bundled up again and stepped out into the crisp March air. The sky remained a dull steel, but the wind had died down, making the walk toward the quiet grounds more pleasant. As they passed through the central courtyard near the entrance of the park, Ellen noticed Sue walking briskly, her boots clapping on the sidewalk ahead of them.

"Look at you go," Ellen called.

Sue grinned over her shoulder. "Blackfeet Casino, baby. Three months on that casino floor and I've got calves like a ballerina."

"I wouldn't go *that* far," Tanya teased.

After the security guard let them inside, they followed the winding path toward the far side of the park where the windmill loomed. The ancient structure looked somehow taller in the cloudy light, its blades barely moving, its weathered wood gray as bone.

As they drew near, the whispering began.

It wasn't loud, just barely audible but unmistakable. The murmurs wrapped around them like a current of invisible thread.

Ellen paused. "Do you hear that?"

"Yeah," Tanya said quietly. "Same as before. Maybe stronger."

Sue pulled her coat more closely around her. "Let's get started."

They each rummaged in their purses for the smaller equipment they always had on them. Tanya pulled out a small EVP recorder, Sue a handheld EMF reader, and Ellen a Mini Maglite flashlight, along with a portable spirit box with a built-in speaker.

Sue flipped on the EMF. The needle hovered at zero.

They formed a small triangle just outside the windmill door. The whispers rose and fell, never forming words, but somehow charged with presence.

Ellen took a breath. "My name is Ellen. These are my friends Tanya and Sue. We're here to help. Not to harm."

"We use these devices," Sue added, "to talk to those who've passed on. If you want to speak with us, you can use the spirit box or the flashlight."

Ellen turned on the spirit box. The static buzz filled the air, crackling like a distant storm. "Is anyone here?"

A pause.

"Can you give us a sign?" Sue added. "Your name?"

Then, through the crackle: *"Al."*

Ellen's head jerked up. "Did you hear that?"

Tanya nodded slowly. "Al. Short for Alfred?"

"Hmm," Ellen began. "Alfred Wilkes? Is that you?"

"That seems too easy," Sue pointed out. "Maybe Albert or Alfonso."

More static. Then a burst of syllables they couldn't make out. It could've been a different language—or just noise. Hard to say.

"Can you give us another name?" Sue asked. "Or a word?"

No reply. The static continued.

Ellen glanced at the EMF reader. No spike.

Tanya tried again. "Do you remember the shipwreck? The *Sea Wren*? Can you tell us what happened?"

Nothing but hissing static.

For the next hour, they moved through different spots around the windmill, trying various questions, switching devices, even going completely silent to allow space for ambient response. But other than the name "Al," they got nothing intelligible.

Finally, Sue groaned and buttoned her coat higher. "I think they're either shy or messing with us."

"Or maybe we're not asking the right questions," Ellen murmured. Still, disappointment prickled in her gut. That name—Al—had felt so promising.

"Let's take a lap around the park," Tanya suggested. "Check for temperature drops or EMF spikes. Maybe we'll get more in one of the houses."

Sue strapped her purse over her shoulder. "As long as we don't have to climb anything."

"I thought you had calves like a ballerina?" Tanya teased.

"But feet and knees like a time-worn sailor," Sue said with a lift of her brows.

They walked the path again, soon coming upon Cotswold Cottage, Ellen's favorite building because she adored the English cottage look, and this one did not disappoint.

"Why don't we sit at the tea table in the courtyard for a moment?" Ellen suggested.

"I want a garden like this," Tanya said as they took their seats. "It's pretty even before the spring flowers have bloomed."

"Would you invite us over for tea?" Sue teased.

"Of course. Though I doubt it would be as nice as this."

Ellen took out her spirit box and attempted to make contact, but after several minutes, gave up.

"Shall we move on?" Sue asked, climbing to her feet.

Next, they approached the Noah Webster House. Once again, their instruments didn't pick up on any unusual activity.

Tanya stopped before a placard. "To prepare himself for studying the origin of words, Webster learned twenty different languages and their alphabets."

"That's interesting," Ellen commented as she caught up to her friend.

Sue, who was ahead of them, said, "My EMF detector is picking up something over here. This is the Robert Frost House."

"My favorite poet!" Ellen said, as she eagerly caught up with Sue. "I have collections containing every poem he ever wrote."

"Is anyone here?" Sue called out. "We come in peace, to help, not harm. We want to help you move on to the other side."

Ellen pulled out her spirit box. "Is Robert Frost here with us, by any chance?" Then she added, "Two roads diverged in a yellow wood, and sorry I could not travel both, and being one traveler, long I stood—"

"Stop showing off," Tanya scolded.

The word, "Yes," came over the box, causing Ellen to flinch with excitement. "Oh, my gosh," she whispered. "Do you think it could be him? *The* Robert Frost?"

This time, the word, "No," came clear and unmistakable over her device.

"Someone's messing with us," Tanya muttered.

"Do you know why the windmill is whispering?" Sue asked.

The word, "No," came through the device.

"Do you have a message for us?" Ellen asked.

This time, the word, "Okay," came though.

"We're listening," Sue encouraged.

Nearly a minute went by without another coherent word.

"Why are you here?" Tanya prompted.

The three friends listened to the device for another minute, but no more words were audible.

"Let's move on," Sue suggested.

Across the street was the Edison Homestead, where Sue, once again, picked up on some activity.

"It's spiking red!" Sue cried excitedly.

They stepped inside where they found a modest, wood-framed interior with simple 19th-century furnishings, including hand-hewn beams, rustic wooden floors, and a cast-iron stove in the kitchen.

"I get a vibe in here," Tanya said softly.

Ellen didn't speak. She stepped forward, walking slowly toward the chair by the window. A cold draft, like the one she'd felt in Henry Ford's home, crawled across her skin. She held up the Mini Maglite and placed it on a table.

"If there's anyone here with us," she said gently, "can you turn on the flashlight?"

They waited. Five seconds. Ten. The beam stayed off.

But then the EMF reader spiked again.

Sue held it up for the others to see. "There!"

Tanya leaned in. "Two point five, then back to zero."

"Someone's here," Ellen whispered.

Sue glanced around the room, now visibly uneasy. "We're here to help, not harm."

"Can you turn on the light?" Ellen asked again.

The flashlight flickered.

Ellen smiled. "Thank you. Can you turn it off now?"

It dimmed. Then went out.

Tanya clutched her notebook, her eyes wide. "Okay, now *that's* a response."

"Can you tell us your name?" Ellen asked, pressing "record" on the EVP device.

No audible response. But the air grew colder.

"Maybe we're not dealing with just one spirit," Tanya whispered. "Maybe something bigger is anchoring them all here."

Just then, the old phonograph on a nearby shelf—an artifact that shouldn't even be functional—crackled to life and emitted a high-pitched, scratchy voice that said, "Hello, hello, hello!" The sound was unmistakably mechanical, yet eerily urgent. The temperature dropped in the room, and the rocking chair in the corner began to creak and sway, though no one stood near it.

The three friends stared at one another, wide-eyed. Without a word, they bolted for the door, the phonograph still crackling behind them.

CHAPTER SIX

The Visitor

The March wind slapped against Ellen's coat as she tugged it tighter around her shoulders, her gloved hand fumbling with the buttons. The Model T chugged and sputtered as John Coleman pulled it up to the curb in front of the Henry Ford Museum, its headlights cutting through the early evening gloom. Ellen, Tanya, and Sue clambered in, Tanya up front again, laughing as she adjusted her ponytail. Ellen slid across the back seat beside Sue.

Why had they run? She and her friends had come to talk to ghosts, not to run from them. But something about that phonograph moving on its own had been too much.

"You ladies warm enough?" John asked, glancing in the rearview mirror.

"Just barely," Tanya answered cheerfully. "This Texas blood wasn't made for Michigan springs."

Sue grumbled, shifting in her seat. "I still think that windmill stirred something up. I've been cold since we left it."

Ellen opened her mouth to respond, but the words stuck in her throat.

She froze. Not from the cold.

Something shifted in the space between her and Sue. A pressure. A weight in the air.

She turned her head slowly, glancing into the rearview mirror perched just above John's cap.

And saw them.

Two disembodied red eyes. Hovering in the darkened space behind them. No face, no outline—just those eyes, glowing faintly, like embers in the dark.

She glanced behind her, wondering if there were red lights in the distance causing an illusion. Nothing.

Her heart thudded loudly as the hair on the back of her neck stood straight up.

"Everything okay back there?" John asked, as he eased the Model T around a corner.

"Mmhmm," Ellen murmured, eyes still locked on the mirror. She forced a tight smile, hoping Sue wouldn't notice her stiff posture.

Tanya and John chatted about the day's tour—favorite buildings, the chill of the air, how quiet the park had felt. But Ellen stayed silent. She could still *feel* it. Whatever it was, it wasn't content to linger at Greenfield Village.

It had followed them.

By the time John dropped them off in front of the Patrick Henry House, the red eyes had vanished from the mirror, but the sensation lingered—like being watched by someone just out of view.

She didn't mention it as they thanked John and made their way up the short path. The porch light glowed warmly, and the solid brass doorknob felt oddly comforting under her palm.

Inside, they shed their coats and boots and moved into the front sitting room.

Then Ellen paused.

She still felt it.

The air had changed. Thickened.

Sue turned, her expression tight. "Okay, is it just me, or does it feel like someone came inside with us?"

Tanya raised an eyebrow. "You too?"

Ellen nodded slowly. "I saw red eyes. In the Model T."

Sue's face paled. "Red eyes?"

"In the rearview mirror. Just for a second. But I'm telling you, something's still here."

Tanya looked around, then motioned toward the sitting room's central coffee table. "Should we try to make contact?"

Ellen nodded. "Let's not wait."

They moved with practiced coordination. From their bags came a spirit box, a Mini Maglite, EMF meter, and their full-spectrum cameras. Ellen retrieved three white candles from the mantel and lit them with a long match, placing them in a circle on the antique coffee table.

The flames danced, casting flickering shadows along the walls.

"You wearing your tourmaline ring?" Ellen asked quietly.

"Always," Tanya said.

Sue patted her chest. "*Gris gris* bag, too."

"Good," Ellen said, settling into the armchair. "Let's start."

The spirit box whirred to life, static crackling as it cycled rapidly through frequencies. The Mini Maglite rested on the table, turned just slightly off—a method they used often to let spirits tap the bulb to "yes" or turn it off for "no."

"Spirit who followed us," Ellen said, voice steady, "are you here in peace?"

A faint knock echoed from the corner of the room. Not from the house itself—but from *inside* the room. The Maglite flickered once. Then held.

"Was that you?" Sue asked. "If so, please knock once for yes or twice for no."

A single knock.

Ellen took a breath. "Do you mean us harm?"

Silence.

Then two knocks, short and rapid. The Maglite flickered off.

"No," Tanya whispered.

"Do you need our help?" Ellen asked.

A single knock. Firm and clear. The Maglite flickered on.

"Yes," Tanya said with a nod.

Ellen looked at her friends. "Okay," she said softly. "We're listening."

Tanya reached over and turned up the volume on the spirit box. The static roared louder. At first, just noise—typical for the early minutes.

Then, faint and crackled: "Hello. Hello. Hello."

All three women sat up straighter.

"Was that you?" Ellen asked. "Did you say hello?"

"Yes," came the reply—crisp and unmistakable.

Tanya leaned forward. "Can you tell us your name?"

A pause. Static. Then: "Listen."

They waited. Another burst of garbled sound. To Ellen, it almost sounded like, "Mary had a little lamb." Then, one word, clean and clear: "Al."

"Al?" Sue repeated. "That's it?"

Ellen exchanged glances with Tanya. "Al, are you the one we sensed at Edison's Homestead?"

A quiet "Yes," came through.

"Did you follow us back here?" Ellen asked.

"Yes."

"Do you have a message for us?" Tanya added.

The reply came fast this time. "Help."

Ellen swallowed. "We want to help. What's your full name?"

The box hissed with static. Then a faint, unintelligible phrase.

"What was that?" Sue asked.

"Say it again," Ellen requested gently.

Another garbled burst. Then, clear as a bell: "Edison."

Tanya blinked. "Edison?"

Ellen felt the air still around them. "Al Edison?" she asked slowly.

"Are you related to Thomas Edison?" Sue added.

A brief pause.

"Me," the box said.

The flames of the three candles shuddered all at once.

Ellen leaned in. "Are you *Thomas Edison*?"

"Yes."

The room fell deathly silent for a heartbeat.

Sue let out a small gasp. "Then . . . who's Al?"

"Me."

"Wait," Tanya said, grabbing her phone. Her fingers flew across the screen. "Hold on . . oh, my gosh! His full name was Thomas *Alva* Edison. His family called him Al."

Ellen sat back, stunned. "We've been talking to Edison."

Sue blinked. "I can't believe it. Why would he come to us?"

Ellen shook her head. "I don't know. But he said he needs help."

Tanya stared at the spirit box. "If Thomas Edison's ghost is reaching out to us, there's got to be a reason."

"We should ask what kind of help he needs," Sue said, already leaning forward.

But the spirit box hissed violently, the static intensifying into a near whine. All three women covered their ears, and the Maglite burst into full light.

Then the static dropped off, and everything went silent.

Dead silent.

Ellen looked around. The candles still flickered. The EMF meter blinked but held steady.

She reached forward and clicked off the spirit box.

Tanya's face was pale. "Did he cut the connection?"

"Or something pulled him away," Ellen murmured.

Sue folded her arms. "That was . . . intense."

Ellen exhaled. "We need to dig deeper into his history. If this really is Thomas Edison, there's probably more going on than just a haunted windmill."

"Way more," Tanya agreed. "But at least we know who we're dealing with now."

Ellen blew out the candles. The last tendrils of smoke curled into the air, vanishing into the shadows.

The spirit had left—for now.

But the mystery of the whispering windmill had just gotten a whole lot stranger.

CHAPTER SEVEN

The Whitney

Why didn't I look up good places to eat before now?" Sue asked, frowning down at her phone as she scrolled aimlessly through map results. "This Zepbound has me thinking less and less about food, but we're in one of the most haunted cities in America, and I've got no clue where we might dine with some otherworldly company."

They sat in the sitting room of the Patrick Henry House after just having scoured their full-spectrum cameras and EVP recorder for evidence. They hadn't captured anything more than what they had already heard during their session with what they believed was the ghost of Thomas Edison.

"Honestly," Ellen replied, her voice still laced with the chill of their recent encounter, "I could use a little normalcy. Maybe even white tablecloths and candles that *aren't* part of a séance."

"Oh, come on, Ellen," Sue objected. "It's why we're here."

Tanya glanced up from her phone. "For once, I agree with Sue. Sometimes ghosts talk to each other, and you never know when one of them could give us a lead."

"That leaves me outvoted," Ellen said with an exaggerated sigh. "But I suppose you're right."

"I'm Googling places now," Sue said.

"You know, we could ask that Uber driver from yesterday," Tanya suggested. "What was his name? C.W.?"

Sue's eyes lit up. "Do you still have his card?"

Tanya reached into her oversized purse and rummaged around. With a triumphant grin, she held up the small, black card with gold lettering. "As a matter of fact, I do."

Within moments, Tanya had fired off a quick text. Ellen and Sue leaned in as she read the reply aloud: "The Whitney, but without reservations on a Thursday night, it could be tricky. Let me pull some strings. I'll pick you up in thirty minutes."

The three women exchanged delighted glances and scattered to freshen up.

Thirty minutes later, Ellen peeked through the front sitting room window. Headlights pulled into the drive, illuminating the frosted glass of the Patrick Henry House.

"He's here!" Tanya called down the hallway.

Sue's voice echoed from the master bathroom. "I need five more minutes!"

"The queen takes her time," Ellen muttered with a fond smile.

Eventually, the trio descended the porch steps and climbed into C.W.'s white SUV. Tanya claimed her usual front seat.

"Ladies," C.W. greeted with a nod, his burly form bundled in a black jacket. His long, dark hair fell across his shoulders. "I hope your ghost hunt didn't scare you off Detroit for good."

"Actually," Ellen said, settling into the back, "we think we made contact with Thomas Edison."

C.W.'s eyes widened in the rearview mirror. "Now that's a name. You know, there wouldn't *be* a Detroit without Edison and Henry Ford. They were good friends. Built this city from the ground up."

Tanya twisted in her seat. "I didn't realize they were close."

"Oh yeah," C.W. said. "Ford idolized Edison. That whole Greenfield Village? Built to honor him."

C.W. went on to share many interesting facts about Detroit—how it was originally occupied by the Ojibwe and then later colonized by the French, led by explorer Antoine de la Mothe Cadillac, who sought permission from King Louis XIV to establish a French outpost, which he called Detroit, mainly for the fur trade. "There's a statue of Antoine de la Mothe Cadillac, along with a memorial of the fifty-five pioneers who founded the city, in Hart Plaza, not far from here."

He went on to say that after a fire razed the city in 1804, two men rebuilt it based on the city of Paris. "One was a French priest, Father Gabriel Richard, the first Catholic priest to be elected to congress. The other was a judge, Augustus Woodward."

"I thought you said the city was built by Henry Ford and Thomas Edison?" Sue challenged.

"Yes," C.W. admitted. "But the groundwork was laid by the other two."

As he spoke, the SUV slowed in front of a grand, turreted mansion bathed in warm exterior lighting. The Whitney.

"If your table's not ready yet," C.W. said, "go upstairs to the Ghost Bar. It used to be the art gallery. The architecture alone is worth the visit."

"Ghost Bar?" Ellen repeated.

"Lots of paranormal activity in this building," he replied.

"You're the best," Sue said, reaching for her wallet.

"Nope," C.W. replied, "I won't hear of it."

But the ladies insisted, giving him not only a tip but their heartfelt thanks.

Inside, the hostess greeted them with a polished smile. "We'll have your table in about fifteen minutes."

"Perfect," Ellen said. "We'll wait upstairs at the bar."

They crossed the opulent main foyer toward the grand staircase. As they passed the large dining room, the antique sconces flanking a clock above the mantle began to flicker.

Ellen stopped. "Do those lights always do that?"

The hostess, just a few steps behind, tilted her head. "Not that I've ever seen. Those sconces are original—installed by Thomas Edison himself."

The three friends exchanged baffled looks before heading upstairs.

The Ghost Bar was a stunning space with gilded ceilings, stained glass, and oil paintings that peered down at them like silent judges. They chose a quiet corner at the far end.

Sue waved over the bartender. "Three glasses of red wine, please—whatever you recommend. We've earned it."

Ellen excused herself and made her way toward the restrooms, just left of the bar.

The restroom antechamber was a luxurious parlor in itself, filled with antique couches, a fireplace, and a dressing vanity.

On one of the sofas sat a woman dressed in 19th-century attire—high collar, silk skirts, and an elaborate brooch.

She was clutching her throat and frowning.

Ellen took a step forward. "Are you okay?"

The woman slowly shook her head, eyes pleading.

Ellen bent over her. "Can I help? Do you need some water?"

A nod.

Ellen hurried back to the bar. "Could I get a glass of water? There's a woman in the lounge who looks like she might faint."

Water in hand, she returned to the parlor—but the woman was gone.

"Hello?" Ellen called softly, walking past the empty stalls. Nothing.

Unnerved, she finished her business and rejoined her friends.

"Did either of you see a woman in period clothing leave the restroom?"

Both shook their heads.

Before Ellen could explain, the hostess appeared. "Your table is ready."

They followed her down one floor to the second level, to a room that the hostess said once belonged to Mrs. Whitney. It was softly lit and intimate, with only four tables.

The antique fireplace crackled quietly. Ellen stilled when she noticed the painting above the mantel. It was the woman from the restroom. She was even wearing the same clothes.

"We're literally dining in someone's bedroom," Tanya whispered.

"At least the ghosts are well dressed," Ellen murmured.

"What are you talking about?" Sue asked.

Ellen quickly relayed her bathroom encounter to her friends.

Their waiter arrived just as she'd finished. "Good evening, ladies. Are we celebrating anything?"

"There's always a reason to celebrate," Sue replied with a wink.

"What would you recommend from the menu?" Ellen asked, trying to distract the waiter from Sue's flirtatious grin.

"I recommend the Beef Wellington. Best in the city."

Ellen and Tanya agreed. Sue batted her lashes and ordered the same, asking for another round of red wine.

"It's a good thing we're not driving," Tanya murmured as she took another sip from her glass.

Ellen leaned across the table. "I meant to ask earlier . . . Have you smoothed things over with Tom?"

"He's wearing me down," Sue admitted. "I told him the only way I'd agree to sell the Montana house is if he agrees to buy another vacation house someplace else. He said we could as long as it's not near a casino. I don't blame him. Even now, the Mo Mummy machine is all I can think about."

"Even more than your grandchildren?" Tanya asked with a tone of disapproval.

"Shep and Lily don't like me anyway," Sue said with a frown. "All they say when Tom and I visit is Pop, Pop, Pop."

"That's not true, I'm sure," Ellen said after taking another sip of her wine.

"They call Stephen's dad P.J.," Sue added. "And they love him, too. Pop and P.J. are all they talk about. And now P.J. plans to take the grandkids to the beach all summer, so who knows when I'll get to see them next?"

"It's too bad Stephen's mom died before they were born," Tanya said gently. "I wonder what they would have called her."

"I don't know, but if they liked her and not me, I'd be a mess," Sue said.

"Maybe P.J. and Tom should become brother-husbands, and that way you can all be with your grandkids at the same time," Ellen teased.

"I like that idea," Sue said with a grin. "Tom and P.J. could sleep together and I could have a room to myself."

The three friends laughed.

"You know," Ellen began, "you're addicted to the gambling because it gives you rushes of dopamine. You just need to find something else that triggers the same kind of rush."

"Like what?" Sue wanted to know.

"Well," Ellen took off her crocheted beanie. "What about crochet? I started several months ago with baby blankets for my grandkids. Then, for Christmas, I made beanies and matching scarves for Brian and the kids. It really does give me a rush when I finish something, and it's not hard to learn."

"I feel the same way about knitting," Tanya put in.

Sue frowned. "Somehow I doubt that the rush you get from yarn is as powerful as the one I get when Mo Mummy hits the grand."

Ellen sighed and returned her beanie to her head.

Tanya pulled out her notebook. "Let's get back to the investigation."

"We need to learn everything we can about Edison," Ellen said with a nod.

Sue pulled out her phone and texted John Coleman. "Private tour of Menlo Lab with a guide who knows Edison inside and out?"

Seconds later, John replied: "I know just the man. Shall I pick you up at 10:15 tomorrow?"

Sue showed the text to the others. "We're in."

Just then, their entrees arrived, piping hot and beautifully plated.

The Beef Wellington was everything they'd hoped for—tender, buttery, and rich with flavor.

Sue raised her wine glass. "Here's to getting to know our friend, Thomas Edison, much better than we ever thought we would."

They clinked glasses.

The sconces over the fireplace flickered.

CHAPTER EIGHT

Menlo Lab

The next morning dawned cold and clear, the Michigan sky a pale, icy blue. Ellen took one more sip of coffee before following Sue and Tanya from the Patrick Henry House. She hadn't slept well, uneasy about their paranormal visitor. A moment later, a black Ford Explorer pulled up to the curb, the Ford logo gleaming in the morning light.

"Well, this is an upgrade," Sue quipped, eyeing the vehicle.

John Coleman rolled down the window and grinned. "Thought we'd give the Model T a break. Climb in. We've got a special tour waiting."

Ellen hated to admit it, but the drive to Greenfield Village was more pleasant in the modern vehicle, especially with the heated seats. The park, however, still closed to tourists, was quiet and almost eerie. Snow clung to the roofs of the historic buildings, and aside from a few bundled-up maintenance workers clearing paths, the village was deserted.

John stopped near a large, barn-like building with a peaked roof and tall windows. A sign out front read: Menlo Park Laboratory.

"Call me when you're ready to be picked up," John said as the three friends climbed out.

A heavyset man in his forties stood waiting by the entrance. He wore a thick, brown coat, fingerless gloves, and a Ford ID badge clipped to his collar.

"You must be the Ghost Healers," he said, his voice a rich baritone. "I'm Leroy. I'll be your docent today."

They introduced themselves, and Leroy pushed open the lab's door. The inside smelled of old wood, machine oil, and history.

"This building is a reconstruction of Edison's original lab from Menlo Park, New Jersey," Leroy said as they stepped into the main floor. "Brought here piece by piece. This was ground zero for some of his biggest breakthroughs."

The space was crammed with wooden tables, shelves of glassware, and old machinery.

"When Henry Ford revealed to Edison his plans to bring Menlo Lab to Dearborn, Tom said he thought the lab should remain on New Jersey soil," Leroy continued. "So, Ford brought over seven truckloads of New Jersey soil for the building's foundation."

"How funny," Sue commented as they looked around the building.

"Ford was always doing things like that for Edison," Leroy explained. "He gave his sons new cars and loaned money to Edison that he never expected to get back. Ford worshipped the man, and rightly so. While Edison didn't create the first light bulb, he did invent the first usable one and literally was responsible for lighting up the world."

In the center of the room sat a curious device with a horn-shaped mouthpiece and a rotating cylinder.

"This," Leroy said reverently, "is a replica of Edison's original phonograph, the invention that made him famous long before the incandescent light bulb."

He picked up a small, tin sheet covered in wax. "The story goes, he was toying with the idea of recording sound. As he spoke into the mouthpiece, this vibrating needle etched grooves into tinfoil wrapped around this cylinder. When Edison cranked the shaft and ran the needle over the grooves, he heard his own voice, the very first recording."

"So, we have Edison to thank for the music record industry?" Tanya asked.

"Indeed, we do," Leroy replied. "And the talking film industry. His film company created the first talkies."

Leroy leaned over the device and turned a crank. Then, into the horn, he spoke:

"Hello, hello, hello. Mary had a little lamb; its fleece was white as snow. And everywhere that Mary went, the lamb was sure to go."

Ellen froze. Her breath caught as chills ran down her spine. She turned to Sue and Tanya—both wide-eyed. Those were the exact words they'd heard the day before over the spirit box.

Leroy chuckled, oblivious. "Those are the words Edison used in his demos. Gave people goosebumps back then too."

Sue crossed her arms. "Have you or anyone else ever experienced anything paranormal in this lab, or in any of the other buildings?"

"I haven't, but my friend Bob, another docent, swears he's seen a shadow man wearing a hat. He's convinced it's Edison's ghost." Leroy shrugged. "I've never seen it."

Ellen glanced at her friends. She'd told them about the incident reports and they'd commented on the hat man. Could he be Edison?

Leroy led them up a narrow staircase to the second floor, where shelves lined every wall, holding hundreds of glass jars and vials.

"Edison believed in being ready for anything," Leroy explained. "These shelves held all sorts of substances and chemicals—he once said he wanted to be able to create any compound his experiments might require, without leaving the lab."

"Was he really that prepared?" Sue asked, peering at a row of labels: benzene, ether, mercury. But also copper wire, metal discs, nuts and bolts, and screws.

"He was obsessed," Leroy said. "A true workaholic. He never retired. He continued working into his eighties. He even built housing nearby for his team—mostly bachelors—so they could live and work on site. The boarding house is here in the village, too."

He paused by a display of early light bulbs, then moved to a timeline etched into the wall.

"He didn't just invent. He fought battles too, like the electric current war. Edison promoted direct current. Charles Westinghouse and Nikola Tesla championed alternating current. Edison feared AC was too dangerous. But in the end, he lost that battle."

"What's that over there?" Sue pointed to a wooden chair with straps and electric wiring.

Tanya raised an eyebrow. "The electric chair? Did Edison invent it?"

Leroy hesitated. "Yes—and no. Edison personally opposed the death penalty, but he also wanted to prove how deadly alternating current could be. He figured if executions used it, people might turn against Westinghouse, his primary competitor."

He walked over to the strange-looking wooden chair fitted with copper restraints and leather straps.

"This is a reconstruction of the first electric chair, one of our newest arrivals. Many of its parts are original. Edison's people helped to design and build it. The first man executed in it was William Kemmler. It was supposed to be more humane than hanging, which was Edison's main reason for designing it."

"But it wasn't, was it?" Ellen asked softly as she stared somberly at the torture device.

Leroy shook his head. "Kemmler suffered. They botched it. It took two jolts and several horrible minutes. Reporters said he burned, and witnesses were sick by the smell of burning flesh. George Westinghouse said afterward, 'They could have done better with an axe.'"

"That's a story I could have done without," Sue said with her brows lifted. "If I have nightmares, it'll be your fault, Leroy."

"As you know, history isn't always pleasant," he said without showing any signs of remorse.

Ellen shivered as a chill crept down her spine. Something about the chair, something dark and heavy, tugged at her. "You said this reconstruction is a new arrival?"

"Came in last August, acquired by our curator, George Flint. He added it to the exhibit to broaden the story of Edison's moral conflicts."

Sue and Tanya exchanged glances with Ellen.

"Did I hear my name?" a voice came from the stairs, along with the sound of footsteps. Then, a man emerged from the stairwell. He looked to be in his early sixties, with a white, short beard, round, metal spectacles, and small, brown eyes.

"Hello, George," Leroy greeted. "I was just telling the Ghost Healers about your newest acquisition."

"Indeed," George said with a friendly nod. "It was an excellent find. I'm quite proud of it."

"Do you think it has anything to do with the whispering windmill?" Tanya asked her friends.

"I mean," Sue began, "the timing's right."

Ellen's stomach turned. "What if bringing the chair here stirred something up? Maybe that's what Edison's spirit is trying to tell us."

"I suppose it's possible," George said with a frown.

Leroy looked intrigued. "You know, that's not the only strange story we've had about Edison."

He pulled out his phone and tapped for a moment, then held up the page of an internet archive. "In 1948, *The Diary and Sundry Observations of Thomas Alva Edison* was published, and the final chapter focused on 'The Realms Beyond.' This chapter was later omitted from subsequent editions because it details Edison's last invention, a device he called a necrophone, which the publishers believed would discredit Edison and why they later left that chapter out."

"A necrophone?" Ellen leaned closer. "A device to . . . what . . . talk to the dead?"

Leroy nodded. "In the book, Edison explains that if our personalities lived on after death, that our memories must, too. He said it seemed only logical that our spirits would want to get in touch with those we left behind. He wanted to build a sensitive device that could record messages from the dead."

Sue let out a breath. "Do you think Edison really invented such a device? Or was that a hoax?"

"It sounds incredible to me," George said. "I wouldn't put any stock into it."

"I disagree." Leroy tucked his phone away. "The spiritualist movement was booming back then. Séances, mediums, spirit photography. I believe it's legit."

Ellen looked at her friends. Their expressions mirrored her own sense of urgency.

"We need to find a copy of that book," she said.

Tanya nodded. "And see if that necrophone ever made it off the page."

Sue glanced back at the electric chair, her voice hushed. "If Edison wanted to speak to the dead, maybe he still does."

They fell silent, the echoes of history swirling around them.

Outside, the wind picked up, rattling the windows. Somewhere in the distance, a faint mechanical whir spun through the air—like a phonograph just beginning to turn.

CHAPTER NINE

The Diary and Sundry Observations of Thomas Alva Edison

The coffee shop near Greenfield Village smelled of cinnamon and dark roast. Snow drifted lazily past the windows, frosting the edges of the glass as Ellen, Sue, and Tanya settled into a booth near the front. A young barista brought their sandwiches—turkey cranberry, grilled cheese, and a towering club—along with three steaming mugs of coffee.

Ellen opened her phone and connected to the shop's Wi-Fi. Her heart still buzzed with the electricity of their tour at Menlo Lab. Leroy's stories, especially about Edison's final, secretive invention—the so-called "necrophone"—had set her nerves dancing. Now, she wanted proof. Real proof.

"Here it is," she said, tapping on a link to the Internet Archive. "The 1948 edition of *The Diary and Sundry Observations of Thomas Alva Edison*, edited by Dagobert D. Runes." She skimmed the opening pages. "These first pages are really just records of his day—a literal diary." She scrolled through more. "Okay, in this next section he says that his deafness helped rather than hindered his life experiences. His refuge was the

Detroit Public Library where he read the entire collection. He claims that his deafness was even an advantage as a telegrapher, his earliest job."

"Go to the final chapter," Tanya prompted.

"Okay." Ellen scrolled through the book to the end. "Here it is: 'The Realms Beyond.'"

Sue slid her tray aside and leaned in. Tanya adjusted her readers and sipped her coffee. The three friends fell silent as Ellen began to read aloud:

"'The real reason for my interest in communication with the beyond,'" Ellen read, "'is a personal one. I do not propose to elaborate here, save to say that if such a thing is possible, it must be approached through scientific means, not through séances and so-called mediums.'"

"Sounds like a snob to me," Sue commented.

Tanya cocked her head to the side. "Yes, he does, but the point is, he believed the afterlife was possible, and he wanted to build a machine to prove it. Something measurable."

Sue nodded, her brow furrowed. "I still can't believe I've never heard this before. Thomas Edison, one of the most famous inventors in history, trying to build a phone to talk to the dead?"

Ellen scrolled further and continued reading, "'I have always said that if our personality survives, it is strictly logical or scientific to assume it retains memory, intellect, and other faculties. Therefore, if personality exists after what we call death, it is reasonable to conclude that those who have passed on may wish to communicate with those still in the flesh.'"

"This wasn't some passing curiosity," Ellen pointed out. "He kept notes. Diagrams. Ideas."

They passed the phone between them, reading in turns, pausing now and then to point out phrases, the text growing stranger and more fascinating with each paragraph.

"'Life is indestructible,'" Ellen read aloud, her voice soft but resonant. "'It does not cease at death, but rather continues, transformed or relocated, through different channels and states.'"

Sue's eyebrows rose. "He sounds more like a meta-physicist than an inventor."

"Or a philosopher," Tanya added before sipping her coffee.

Ellen nodded and read on, "'An individual, as we understand the term, is not a singular organism, but a community of infinitesimal units of life—intelligent entities that cooperate in harmony to form what we perceive as a man.'"

"That's fascinating," Tanya murmured. "Cellular theory meets spiritualism."

Ellen scrolled further, her eyes scanning the screen. "Listen to this: 'I observed in Florida a peculiar bush growing in the ocean. Upon closer study, I learned that the bush was no vegetable at all, but rather a construction of animal matter—tiny insects, working collectively to simulate flora. The bush was not a bush. It was a bustling metropolis of coordinated life. I believe the same is true of man.'"

Tanya leaned forward. "He's saying people aren't individuals, they're ecosystems."

"Exactly," Ellen said, reading on. "'When the body dies, the workers do not perish. They disperse. But do they retain a memory of their former configuration? Do they preserve the personality of the being they once composed? This is the question my apparatus endeavors to answer.'"

All three women sat in silence for a beat, the magnitude of the idea settling like dust in the lamplight.

"So, he wasn't just making a ghost detector," Sue said. "He was trying to prove that the personality—the soul, essentially—continues on as a coherent entity."

"And if it does," Tanya said, finishing the thought, "his machine could record it."

Ellen nodded, her heart thudding with excitement. "He didn't want to prove ghosts existed just to shock people. He wanted to provide scientific evidence for life after death."

They read on, fascinated by Edison's detailed speculations. He imagined a device finely tuned to the subtle vibrational frequencies emitted by these post-mortem "units of life." He believed that by capturing their coordinated activity, a coherent message could be extracted.

"'If the swarm of units retains the personality of the whole,'" Ellen read, her voice reverent, "'then it should be able to communicate as that individual once did. This is the crux of my theory—that life after death is not an illusion, but a continuum of organization.'"

Sue, who had pulled up the book on her phone, too, said, "Listen to this: 'I am at work on an apparatus,'" she read, "'which, if successful, will render it possible for those who have passed on to communicate with us. The apparatus will be extremely sensitive to vibrations outside the physical realm.'"

"Did he ever finish it?" Tanya wondered. "Did it work?"

"Let's find out," Ellen said. She opened a new browser tab and typed: Edison necrophone demonstration. After a moment, she gasped. "There's an old newspaper article—*The Newark Gazette*, 1926. It's titled 'Dial a Ghost: Edison Demonstrates Communication with the Dead.'"

"Seriously?" Sue leaned in.

"Read it," Tanya prompted.

Ellen clicked the link and scanned the yellowed, digitized text. "'Thomas A. Edison, famed Wizard of Menlo Park, unveiled what he called a 'necrophone' this Thursday, claiming it capable of capturing and replaying messages from those who have passed on. Demonstrating before a small gathering of colleagues, the device emitted what the inventor called 'residual etheric impressions.''" Ellen paused. "'Attendees described the sounds as indistinct murmurs, while others claimed to hear phrases such as 'I am here' and 'Remember me.''"

"Eerie," Sue whispered. "Like an earlier version of the EVP recorder."

Ellen continued, "'Critics dismissed the experiment as a parlor trick, citing faulty wiring or perhaps Edison's own declining faculties. Nonetheless, the inventor insists he will perfect the machine and unveil it to the public within the year.'"

"But he never did," Tanya said.

"No," Ellen said. "He died in 1931 and, as far as I can tell, never fulfilled that promise."

They sat in silence for a moment, sipping their coffee. Snow thickened outside.

"Do you think that's what's happening now?" Sue asked finally. "The windmill. The whispers. The spirit box saying 'Mary had a little lamb.' That was the same thing Leroy said Edison recorded during his phonograph demonstrations."

"You think Edison is trying to demonstrate his last invention?" Tanya asked Sue.

Ellen nodded. "It fits. Leroy even said the reconstructed electric chair was added just last fall. Maybe that's what stirred things up."

"So, he's trying to finish what he started," Tanya said. "Trying to get his message out. But why now? And why us?"

"We've encountered plenty of ghosts before," Ellen said, her voice thoughtful. "Some angry, some sad, some just . . . stuck. But Edison doesn't seem like any of them. He's trying to communicate something, and not just to any random person."

Sue leaned forward. "We were brought here for a reason. That phone call from John Coleman. The invitation to investigate."

Ellen glanced at them both, her heart pounding. "We're going to need to try to make contact. Again. But this time, with intent."

"You mean, to ask him directly," Tanya said.

Ellen nodded. "Why he's reaching out. Why now. And what he wants us to do."

Sue grinned, that mischievous sparkle returning to her eyes. "Then, it's official. We're going ghost hunting with Edison."

CHAPTER TEN

A Dark Presence

The wind had picked up.

As Ellen, Sue, and Tanya crossed the narrow street in front of the coffee shop, the air carried a damp chill, rattling the last dry leaves clinging to the skeletal trees that lined Greenfield Village. Ellen pulled her coat higher around her neck and clutched her equipment bag tighter as they approached the gates, already open from earlier. A security guard stood just inside, recognized them, and waved them through without a word.

Farris Windmill loomed in the distance like a sentinel against the cloudy sky, its blades creaking slightly in the breeze. The three women walked in silence, their steps falling into rhythm, each of them mentally preparing for what might happen next.

Ellen felt the familiar hum of anticipation coil in her chest. She had done dozens of investigations over the years, but something about this one buzzed differently beneath her skin. Maybe it was the gravity of who they hoped to contact. Or maybe it was the unsettling sense that they weren't the only ones watching this time.

They reached the base of the windmill, its wooden frame gray and weathered, but strong. Ellen bent over and began unpacking their equipment.

Sue picked up a full-spectrum camera. "Let's get eyes on everything."

Tanya had her EVP recorder in hand, slipping on a pair of headphones which she connected to the recorder. "I'm rolling," she said, voice low and tense.

Ellen turned on the spirit box and set it on the stone walkway, the device sputtering to life with static and broken frequencies. Next, she placed the Mini Maglite beside it. Then, finally, she powered up the SLS camera, watching through the screen as the world around them shifted into skeletal, digital lines.

She took a breath and projected her voice. "We are not here to harm or mock you. My name is Ellen. These are my friends, Sue and Tanya. We respectfully ask to speak with Thomas Alva Edison. If you're here with us, please let yourself be known."

For a moment, only static.

Then, a clicking sound. Sharp, deliberate.

A burst of white noise hissed through the spirit box. Then: "Hello. Hello. Hello."

The three women froze.

Sue's eyes widened behind her camera. Tanya looked up from her recorder, nodding slowly.

Ellen swallowed hard as her SLS camera picked up a stick figure standing near the opened door of the windmill tower. "Mr. Edison, if that is you, please confirm by turning on the flashlight."

A second passed.

Ellen saw the figure move from the windmill door towards the Mini Maglite.

The Mini Maglite flickered once, then glowed steadily.

Ellen gasped. "Thank you."

Sue steadied her camera. "Do you have a message for us? Why are you here after having been gone for so long?"

The spirit box crackled. Words began to filter through in short bursts: "Stayed . . . Never gone."

"You were never gone?" Ellen repeated. "If that's true, please turn the flashlight off."

She watched in stunned silence as the Mini Maglite flickered off.

Then, over the spirit box, came more words and phrases: "Paradise on earth . . . Tinkering . . . My lab."

Ellen's chest tightened. "You never left. This is your heaven."

She was reminded of what the ghost of George Vanderbilt had told her at the Biltmore in Asheville a few Christmases ago. He'd remained in his castle for the same reason.

More static came over the spirit box. Then: "Always working."

Tanya leaned forward. "Is something keeping you from your work now? Is that why the windmill is whispering?"

The response took longer to form.

"Darkness."

Ellen and her friends exchanged looks of concern.

"What kind of darkness?" Sue asked. "What does it look like?"

"Red eyes."

The three women glanced at one another once again, eyes wide, mouths open.

Ellen's fingers tightened on the SLS camera. "We thought the spirit who followed us yesterday might have been you, but you're saying something else is here. Something dark."

The flashlight flickered.

Sue's voice was tense. "Mr. Edison, can you tell us more about it? What is this presence?"

"Evil."

A chill slid down Ellen's back.

"Can you prove to us you're Thomas Edison?" Ellen suddenly asked, not sure what to believe anymore. "Tell us something only you would know. Something from your writings, your diary."

The spirit box hissed.

"Life . . . is neither created nor destroyed . . . I was right . . . about that."

Tanya's mouth fell open slightly. "That's what he wrote. The swarm of workers. The theory."

Sue's camera trembled in her hands. "Why is this other presence here, then? What does it want?"

The spirit box whined.

Then, all at once, the static surged, violent and loud.

Next, they heard clicks and bursts of incoherent speech. Then, in a guttural voice unlike the one before: "Help me! I'm in hell!"

The three women stood stock-still.

Ellen's heart thudded in her ears.

"Edison?" she said, voice trembling, no longer able to pick up the stick figure on her SLS camera. "Is that you?"

The Mini Maglite suddenly rolled across the pavement.

It spun to a stop, its beam flashing on and off rapidly—like a strobe.

Then, the spirit box fell silent.

There was utter silence.

Even the wind had stopped, though the blades of the windmill continued to move.

Tanya slowly removed her headphones. "That wasn't Edison at the end, I don't think. I don't know. And, guys, I heard more than one voice. Dozens of them were whispering."

Ellen exhaled, lowering the SLS camera. Her hands were shaking.

The stillness around the windmill was heavy, like air before a storm.

"We need to regroup," Ellen said. "And we need to figure out what that presence is . . . and how to help Edison, if he's trapped here with it."

Tanya looked toward the windmill, the old blades still turning slowly. "And who are the other voices?"

Sue clicked off her camera. "And we need to find out what that thing wants."

Ellen reached down and picked up the flashlight. Its casing was cold.

She looked at her friends, and then back toward the windmill.

The whispering was subtle but still there.

Ellen took a deep breath. "We need to research that electric chair. This dark entity seems to have arrived around the same time it did."

"Good idea," Sue said. "I'll text John to come pick us up."

Ellen and Tanya gathered their equipment while Sue reached out to John. Ellen couldn't shake the feeling that the red eyes in the rearview mirror yesterday had *not* belonged to Edison. Had the dark entity followed them home? And would it do so again?

CHAPTER ELEVEN

A Restless Night

The black Ford Explorer glided through the quiet streets of Dearborn as dusk began to settle over the city. Inside, the atmosphere was thick with contemplation.

Ellen sat in the back seat, her thoughts swirling. The recent encounter at the Farris Windmill had left her unsettled. She leaned forward slightly, breaking the silence. "We forgot to ask the ghost of Thomas Edison about the necrophone."

John Coleman's hands tightened on the steering wheel. "You spoke with the ghost of Thomas Edison?"

Tanya, seated beside him, nodded. "We think so. And possibly something darker, too."

Sue added from the back, "We suspect the dark entity came with the electric chair. Any ideas who or what it might be?"

John shook his head, his expression grave. "You ladies are out of my league, I'm sorry to say." He paused, then added, "I don't know if this is helpful, but in the indoor museum, we have a test tube containing some of Edison's last breath."

Ellen's eyes widened. "How is that possible?"

As John pulled up to the curb in front of the Patrick Henry House, he explained, "Henry Ford asked Edison's son, Charles, to collect his father's dying breaths in several test tubes, so he could keep a part of Edison for posterity."

Tanya turned to him, intrigued. "Where are these test tubes stored?"

"We have an exhibit in the museum. I can show it to you tomorrow, if you'd like."

"We can't tomorrow," Ellen said from the back beside Sue. "We're going to the Eastern Market."

"All work and no play," Sue explained with a grin.

"Of course," John agreed. "I don't expect you to work the case twenty-four-seven."

"Well, that's a relief," Sue said as she began to climb from the vehicle.

"Our test tube of Edison's breath isn't the only one," John said to Tanya as she was about to exit the Explorer. "Two other institutions were each gifted one, and there are currently twenty others in a storage room in the basement of the museum."

Ellen glanced at her friends as she opened her car door. "I'm not sure if that's relevant, but it may be. There could be something connecting Edison's last breath with his ghost."

"Or with the dark thing," Sue added.

They bid John goodnight and entered the Patrick Henry House. The familiar creak of the floorboards greeted them, but something didn't feel right. Ellen paused in the foyer, sensing a subtle shift in the air.

"Do you feel that?" she asked.

Tanya shrugged off her coat. "I'm not sure. It's not as strong as last night."

Sue nodded. "Could be in our heads."

Ellen wasn't convinced but decided not to press the issue. "Let's order some food and read up on the history of the electric chair. It might shed some light on the nature of this dark entity."

As Tanya looked up restaurants on her phone, she remarked, "Did you know that Detroit has the largest Arab American community in the U.S.?"

Sue raised an eyebrow. "You know what that means?"

Ellen, dreading an insensitive reply from her uncensored friend, couldn't help but ask, "What?"

"Good food!" Sue exclaimed with a grin.

Relieved, Ellen chuckled. "True. Baba ghanoush sounds so good, now that you mention it."

"I want chicken shawarma and a salad," Tanya began, "with olives, feta cheese, and vinaigrette dressing."

"I'm not that hungry," Sue admitted, "but a salad sounds good to me, too."

They decided to order Mediterranean food through DoorDash. While waiting, they each pulled up articles on their phones about the electric chair.

Ellen began, "It was conceived by Alfred P. Southwick, a dentist and steamboat engineer. But it might not have come to fruition without Edison's involvement. Southwick sought Edison's opinion on legal electrocution and information on the necessary strength of current to produce death with certainty."

Sue interjected, "Edison initially opposed capital punishment. But Southwick persisted, emphasizing the need for a more humane method than hanging. Eventually, Edison agreed to support the use of electrocution."

Tanya added, "Edison's reputation as an electrician helped sway the legislature in favor of the electric chair."

"Here's a Princeton article about Kemmler," Ellen continued. "Like Leroy told us earlier, the first person executed by electric chair was William Kemmler in 1890. Listen to this: 'The scene of Kemmler's execution was too horrible to picture. Men accustomed to every form of suffering grew faint as the awful spectacle was unfolded before their eyes. Those who stood in the sight were filled with awe as they saw the effects of this most potent of fluids, i.e., electricity, which is only partially understood by those who have studied it most faithfully, as it slowly, too slowly, disintegrated the fiber and tissues of the body through which it passed. The heaving of the chest which, it had been promised, would be stilled in an instant of peace as soon as the circuit was completed, the foaming of the mouth, the bloody sweat, the writhing of shoulders and all other signs of life. Horrible as these all were, they were made infinitely more horrible by the premature removal of the electrodes and the subsequent replacing of them for not seconds but minutes, until the room was filled with the odor of burning flesh and strong men fainted and fell like logs upon the floor.'"

"No more details on that needed," Sue objected. "But it certainly explains why *The New York Times* described the incident as 'far worse than hanging.'"

Tanya found another article. "There have been numerous botched executions since then. For example, in 1990, Jesse Tafero's execution in Florida malfunctioned three times, causing flames to leap from his head."

Ellen shuddered. "That's horrifying."

"Maybe Tafero is the dark entity," Tanya added.

Sue wrinkled her nose. "Don't you think it would be someone who was aware of Edison? I doubt Tafero knew anything about his connection to the electric chair."

Looking at her phone, Tanya said, "My DoorDash app says the food's here. Why don't we take a break and eat?"

The scent of garlic and lemon filled the sitting room of the Patrick Henry House as the three women dug into their Mediterranean feast. Sue had spread a paper napkin across her lap like they were in a fine restaurant, while Tanya balanced her container of chicken shawarma on the arm of the loveseat.

"Oh, my Gawd," Sue moaned with her mouth full, "this salad is delicious."

"Try some of this dip." Ellen held out her container for the others to try.

"Mmm!" Sue agreed.

"I told you," Tanya said, waving a pita triangle in her direction. "Best perk of Detroit—killer food."

They ate for a few moments in peaceful silence until Tanya leaned over and gave Sue a pointed look. "So, you been able to keep your mind off Mo Mummy lately?"

"You bringing it up doesn't help," Ellen said to Tanya.

"Sorry," Tanya muttered before taking another bite.

Sue gave an exaggerated sigh. "No apology necessary. I was already thinking about it. I'm telling you, the grip that slot machine has on me is unholy."

Ellen raised an eyebrow. "Didn't you delete the app?"

"I did!" Sue defended. "But now I just watch people play it on YouTube before bed and when I first wake up in the morning."

Tanya's eyes widened. "I can't believe you're watching other people gamble."

"It's exciting," Sue said. "The music, the bonus rounds, the way Mo pops out and does that little mummy dance when you win big—honestly, it's better than caffeine."

"Well, don't stay up all night," Ellen warned, shaking her pita at her. "We have a big day at Eastern Market tomorrow, remember?"

Sue waved her off. "I'll just watch a few spins. It's not like Mo's gonna rise from the crypt and drag me into a three-hour bonus round or anything."

"That actually sounds on brand for this trip," Tanya said, chuckling. "Hey," Tanya added, nudging Sue. "Now that you've agreed to sell your place on the Blackfeet Reservation, have you thought about where you might want your next vacation house to be?"

Sue dabbed her mouth with her napkin, her expression turning wistful. "Tom and I were thinking Branson, Missouri. No casinos there."

"Branson?" Ellen repeated. "I've never been there."

"You're missing out," Sue said. "Tom and I have been a few times. I love the shows. You've never seen so many sequins in your life. It's like Vegas and a church revival had a very glitzy baby."

Tanya nodded. "Dave and I went there years ago. Must have been five or six years ago—before Covid. We had a great time. The shows are incredible, the food delicious, and the landscape is beautiful. Sounds like a great vacation spot to me."

"I agree," Sue said, looking pleased. "Now I just need to search for the perfect property."

"Something haunted?" Ellen teased.

"Why, of course," Sue replied before taking the last bite of her salad.

They all laughed, the tension of the day easing in the warmth of shared food and silliness. Despite the darkness lingering around their investigation, moments like these reminded Ellen of what grounded them: friendship, humor, and a whole lot of good dip.

"All right," Ellen said, rising to her feet. "Let's get those circles of protection drawn. I'd rather not wake up with Mo Mummy doing a tap dance on my chest."

"Or Edison whispering bedtime trivia into your ear," Tanya added.

"Ugh, I'd take Mo over the ghost of Edison any day," Sue said playfully as she reached for the saltshaker.

"All this talk of Mo," Ellen began, "has me missing my Mose-by-Mo."

"Why didn't you bring him?" Tanya wondered.

"Too cold, I think, especially with the amount of time we're spending outdoors."

"It's not any colder than Telluride in December," Sue pointed out.

"And that was hard on him," Ellen replied.

They got up and went about their bedtime rituals, the echo of laughter still in the air—even as shadows stirred quietly in the corners of the old house.

Ellen turned out the light in the bathroom, toothbrush in hand, and padded back to her bedroom. The warmth from dinner still lingered in her belly, but it had done little to quiet the hum of anxiety beneath her skin. The Patrick Henry House creaked and groaned with every gust of wind outside, as if the walls were breathing—slowly, heavily.

She stepped into her room, shutting the door with a soft click behind her. The antique bed loomed in the center, tall and imposing, its carved posts twisted like vines reaching for the ceiling. She paused to look at it. A beautiful piece of craftsmanship, certainly. But tonight, it felt . . . watchful.

"Don't be ridiculous," she whispered to herself.

Still, her fingers hesitated as she drew a circle of salt on the hardwood floor around the bed. She'd felt that cold draft in the Edison lab. She'd heard the click of the phonograph needle when no one was near it. She'd seen Sue go pale as parchment when the energy in the room turned. Something had followed them.

Whether it was Edison himself or some poor soul executed in one of his machines, she didn't know. But even though it was less obvious than the day before, something was there, she knew it.

When she was done with the salt, she stepped carefully over the circle, uttered the words to close it, and slid into bed, pulling the old quilt up to her chest. The mattress squeaked beneath her weight, its springs protesting. She reached for her phone and checked the time: 11:47 p.m.

From downstairs, she could hear Sue laughing—probably watching Mo Mummy on her phone with the volume too high. The room next door was quiet. Tanya was probably already asleep. Their presence gave Ellen comfort. For all their teasing and bickering, the three of them had grown into something more than friends. Sisters by choice. Partners in haunted real estate. And, in recent years, companions in something stranger still. Ghost healers.

She set her phone on the nightstand and turned out the light. Immediately, the room felt heavier. Not pitch dark—a sliver of moonlight edged in from between the curtains—but dense somehow, like the shadows had weight.

Ellen turned onto her side, pulling the blanket higher.

She told herself the feeling in her chest was just the aftermath of a long day.

But it wasn't exhaustion.

It was dread.

Something *was* in the house. She could feel it. Not close enough to reach her—not yet—but near. Like a cold breath on a windowpane, waiting to fog the glass.

She squeezed her eyes shut.

She thought of Brian and Moseby back home in San Antonio. They'd both be snoring by now. She missed the feel of Brian's arms against hers and the little ball of fur nestled between them.

What would Brian think if he knew that something dark, possibly evil, had followed her and her friends home?

She smiled faintly at the thought, then flinched as the old radiator hissed in the corner.

Just pipes, she reminded herself.

Just the house settling.

But even as she repeated those words, Ellen clutched her *gris gris* bag around her neck, a charm gifted to her by a Voodoo priestess in

New Orleans who claimed it would ward off spirits. Ellen only took it off to shower.

She lay like that for a long time, listening to the sounds of the house. Somewhere downstairs, a floorboard creaked. Outside, the wind rattled the storm windows. A dog barked in the distance—sharp and sudden.

Her thoughts drifted to Edison's final breath, captured in a glass test tube. To the necrophone, humming with an energy that hadn't died with its inventor. To William Kemmler, and that botched execution. The acrid smell of burning flesh. The sparks. The screams.

And what if that suffering had *anchored* something? What if death by electrocution didn't release the soul, but *fused* it to the current?

What if that was what they'd brought back with them?

She rolled to her other side, trying not to think about it. Trying to quiet the anxious loop in her brain. Eventually, her breathing slowed. Her grip on her *gris gris* bag loosened.

Just as sleep began to pull her under, she heard it.

A soft, deliberate tap, as if someone had knocked once on the bedroom wall.

Ellen froze.

She waited. One second. Two. Nothing followed.

Maybe the house, again. Maybe Sue knocked something over. Or maybe—

Her mind, mercifully, tipped into unconsciousness before the thought could finish forming.

But the feeling remained.

Not gone. Just waiting.

CHAPTER TWELVE

The Eastern Market

Ellen leaned against the white-painted railing of the front porch, watching a red squirrel leap between branches overhead. Early sunlight broke across the manicured lawn, and the buzz of bees in the flowerbeds below hummed beneath the quiet morning air. It was warmer than it had been since their arrival.

Tanya tapped on her phone beside her, thumbs flying.

"C.W.'s on his way," Tanya announced with a grin. "Said he just dropped off a couple in Corktown and can be here in fifteen."

Soon enough, a familiar white SUV rolled up to the curb, C.W. waving from behind the wheel with his usual infectious energy. "Ladies! Ready for your next Motor City adventure?"

"We are," Tanya said, sliding into the front seat while Ellen and Sue climbed into the back.

"So, what's the word on the haunted windmill? Still chasing ghosts or did they all move to Florida for retirement?"

Ellen laughed. "We're making progress. We've uncovered more evidence linking Thomas Edison to the site."

"Crazy!" C.W. glanced at her in the rearview mirror.

Tanya turned to him. "There's also an emotional residue. A darkness. We think it's tied to someone who died by the electric chair, maybe unjustly."

C.W. shook his head as he pulled away from the Patrick Henry House. "Well, now you've got to let me drive you past the Eloise on the way home. That place is a whole mood."

"We'd love that," Sue said from the back. "We're always up for a detour down haunted lane."

When they arrived at the Eastern Market, the three women stepped out into a vibrant world of color and scent. Rows of covered sheds stretched into the distance, at least a dozen large pavilions pulsing with life. Vendors offered everything from produce to pottery, from hot sauce to handcrafted jewelry.

"Holy moly," Sue said. "It's like Etsy and Whole Foods had a baby."

"Let's pace ourselves." Ellen shielded her eyes against the morning sun. "This is a marathon, not a sprint."

It didn't take long for the first temptation to strike. Tanya veered toward a stall filled with flowering plants and herbs, crouching beside a pot of deep purple clematis.

Tanya picked up the pot. "I've been looking for this exact variety. Perfect for my back fence."

Ellen tilted her head to the side. "You can't take a plant on a plane."

The vendor overheard. "I can box it up in something TSA-friendly. Air holes and a handle for a carry-on. No problem."

Tanya looked triumphant. "See? The universe wants me to have this clematis."

Ellen shook her head and laughed, then wandered over to a table of handmade clothing. Her fingers brushed over a vest woven from soft wool and silk in rich swirls of midnight blue and charcoal gray. She slipped it on and turned to the mirror.

"That color makes your eyes pop," Tanya said. "The universe wants you to have it."

"Really? The universe?" Ellen mocked, but she bought it anyway.

Sue, meanwhile, was entranced by a leather handbag dyed in shades of burnished gold and garnet. She slung it over her shoulder, checking herself out in a tiny mirror propped up beside the vendor's cash box.

"This would be perfect for the casino," she declared. "Room for snacks, sanitizer, and a lucky rabbit's foot."

"You don't have a rabbit's foot," Tanya said.

"I might buy one," she replied with snark. "I bet someone sells them here. They've got everything else."

Ellen tapped her chin. "I thought the casino was in the past."

"A girl can dream, can't she?" Sue handed the vendor her cash.

They strolled and shopped until their arms were heavy with treasures, then ducked into the Golden Fleece for lunch. The small Greek diner was nestled between a fishmonger and a flower shop. The smell of sizzling lamb, oregano, and garlic drew them inside like sirens.

They ordered gyros with crispy fries and iced tea, claiming a window booth in the back. As they ate, Ellen pulled up an article she'd bookmarked earlier on her phone.

"This is wild," she said, wiping her hands. "It's about Edison and the electric chair. Apparently, after the debacle with Kemmler, Edison blamed the doctors for using electrodes on the skull and leg when he believed bone wouldn't conduct electricity as well as blood. He recommended hand-to-hand electrodes, and because he was the Wizard of Menlo Park, the authorities trusted him."

She began reading aloud from the Princeton article, her voice dipping as she recited the grisly details of the execution, using Edison's method, of nineteen-year-old Charles McElvaine, who had killed a grocer during a robbery gone wrong. "The boy clutched a crucifix in his left hand and prayed aloud to Jesus as his whole body trembled. When the hand-to-hand electrodes failed, MacDonald quickly ordered the skull and leg electrodes to be attached, and McElvaine was then jolted again."

The overhead lights flickered.

Sue looked up, eyes wide. "Did anyone else see that?"

A passing waitress waved it off. "They're doing some construction on the block."

But Ellen felt it—tightness in her chest, a sudden pressure in the air.

"So, the great Thomas Edison was wrong," Sue summarized.

"That poor boy was only nineteen years old," Tanya whispered. "He was still just a kid."

"Well, he did kill someone," Sue reminded her. "But it wasn't nice to make such a young person a guinea pig."

"It bothers me that when they were considering the 'death by electrocution' law, Edison was up there testifying as if he were an expert," Ellen said with exasperation. "Under the scrutiny of a man called Cochrane, Edison admitted on the stand that he knew nothing about human anatomy. That he'd barely seen any relevant experiments."

Tanya sighed. "He was a celebrity being used to push an agenda."

Sue shook her head. "So, after the Kemmler execution went so horribly wrong, Edison blamed the doctors. And everyone believed him because he was famous."

"The papers said that if anyone knew anything about electricity, it was Thomas Edison," Ellen confirmed. "And the authorities gave Edison more credence than doctors."

"I found an article that describes the boy's death," Tanya said, putting a hand over her heart. "'The first contact at 11:15 o'clock was made through the hands and head, and lasted forty-five seconds, the second was through the head and calf of the right leg. A few seconds after the current was cut off of the first contact, froth issued from the mouth, and almost simultaneously there was a quick gurgling sound, and as quick a recovery, like a person strangling. The current was at once reapplied and continued for 45 sec., when the doctors examined the subject and declared him dead.'"

Ellen covered her mouth as tears pricked her eyes.

"I found something, too," Sue began. "One reporter, Arthur Brisbane of *World*, wrote this about McElvaine's death: 'What most repels the spectator at such an execution as that which occurred yesterday, is the sight of a number of men, who have wives and daughters at home and decent associations generally, deliberately occupying themselves with killing a helpless fellow creature.'"

"That poor kid," Tanya said again. "Such unnecessary suffering and a horrible way to die."

As Ellen spoke the name "Charles McElvaine" aloud, the overhead lights flickered again.

Sue looked up and whispered, "That's not the nearby construction."

"He's here with us," Ellen whispered. "I can feel him. Maybe he's the darkness we sensed. Twisted by pain and betrayal. His death wasn't just agonizing. It didn't have to be. But Edison's reputation got in the way."

The lights flickered again. Tanya reached for her phone.

"Let's go back," Sue said, her voice urgent but gentle. "Let's try to talk to him someplace private."

"I'm texting C.W.," Tanya said. "Asking him to pick us up."

Twenty minutes later, they slid back into the SUV, their earlier shopping bags now resting between their feet. C.W. raised an eyebrow in the rearview mirror.

"You all look like you've seen a ghost."

"No, but we felt him," Sue declared.

Ellen remained quiet, staring out the window as the skyline of downtown Detroit faded behind them. The streets thinned. Trees became more numerous, then sparser again as they approached the decaying silhouette of the Eloise Psychiatric Hospital.

Even from the parking lot, the place radiated unease. Tall, narrow windows glared down like eyes. The brickwork was blackened in places, as if the building itself had tried to burn its past away.

C.W. parked near the edge of the cracked pavement and killed the engine. "This is it," he said softly.

"It looks more like a prison," Tanya whispered.

No one moved. Even Sue, usually fearless, reached instinctively for Ellen's hand.

The air outside was still. Heavy. As if something unseen had paused mid-breath, waiting.

Ellen's thoughts returned to Charles McElvaine—terrified, clutching a crucifix, electrocuted in a failed experiment wrapped in the illusion of progress. Was this where his spirit had wandered? A place full of pain and misery?

CHAPTER THIRTEEN

The Eloise

The Eloise wasn't just a building. It was a remnant of a time when the state believed in erecting entire worlds to contain those it didn't understand. Even in its decayed state, the place felt alive.

C.W. turned onto a road that took them near a side entrance. A single figure stood near it, bundled in a black, leather jacket, with brown hair pulled into a tight ponytail beneath a wool hat.

"That's your guide," he said, shifting into park. "Private access. Just you."

Tanya blinked. "Wait—what?"

"She agreed to give you a personal tour. She usually works with production crews or scheduled events, but she's doing me a favor this afternoon."

"That's so nice, but why?" Ellen asked.

"We go to the same church. Basilica of Sainte Anne. I told her about your case—the windmill, the Henry Ford connection, the ghost you think might be Edison. She was intrigued."

Sue smirked. "God bless Detroit Catholics."

The guide introduced herself as Shannon. Appearing to be in her late twenties, she had a flashlight in one hand, a key ring on her belt, and the matter-of-fact demeanor of someone who'd seen enough to skip the theatrics.

"C.W. tells me you're investigating something weird for the Henry Ford Museum," she said as she pushed open a side door. "Weird fits right in here."

"I take it you've worked here a while?" Ellen asked as they stepped into a dark corridor.

"Oh, yes," Shannon said with a laugh.

The air inside was cold and close, like it hadn't been moved in years. Dust motes danced in the flashlight's beam as Shannon led them deeper into the building.

Ellen and her friends pulled out their own flashlights to see by.

"This floor was used for administration," Shannon explained. "When the Eloise was in full operation, there were over seventy buildings—a poor house, asylum, hospital, housing, a bakery, a firehouse, and a post office, to name a few. They sat on nearly a thousand acres, including farmland. This place was its own self-sufficient city."

"Wow," Ellen replied.

"And this building?" Tanya asked.

"One of the newest. Early 1900s."

"It's really something," Sue said.

Shannon continued, "The Eloise is where they brought the patients who didn't respond to traditional treatments—or who didn't have families to claim them."

Tanya shuddered. "Yikes."

Shannon gestured toward a rusted elevator door. "The power doesn't work in most of the building anymore, but if you listen here, sometimes you can hear the elevator ding. No cables, no juice—just echoes."

As if on cue, a soft metallic *ding* echoed from somewhere down the hall.

Tanya froze. "Was that—?"

"I don't fake anything," Shannon said calmly. "Whatever you hear, whatever you see, it's real—or at least, it's not me. Full disclosure, there are two groups in the basement doing our escape room adventures, so if you hear anything, it could be them."

Ellen followed Shannon and her friends up a dark stairwell to the second floor. They passed through a nurses' station and a cracked portrait of Florence Nightingale still hanging askew on the wall.

"This was one of the patient recreation rooms," Shannon said as they stepped into a space lined with collapsed billiards tables and abandoned wheelchairs. There was a television stand in one corner. "There's a theory that spirits are drawn to places that held intense emotions. Think about it—this was where people cried, laughed, hallucinated, died. That energy doesn't just disappear."

Ellen felt a strange pressure in her chest, like something heavy had settled on her sternum. Her eyes darted toward a window—boarded up—and then down a side corridor.

Shannon moved to the center of the room, to a strange-looking chair. "And this over here is an original dental chair to the asylum. Sometimes extracting a patient's teeth was the only way to keep them from biting you."

"Oh, my gosh," Tanya groaned.

"And that's an original treadmill," Shannon pointed to a machine in a corner. "It's pretty rusted. I don't recommend trying it."

They entered another large room with barred windows. A few metal bedframes lined one wall.

"This was one of many common sleeping quarters," Shannon said. "This floor had a capacity for four hundred beds. There must have been a hundred in this room alone."

"A hundred?" Tanya repeated with a look of dismay.

"Exactly," Shannon said with a nervous laugh.

"I feel like we're being watched," Ellen said quietly.

"You are," Shannon replied, flashing a half-smile. "He's usually on this floor."

"Who?" Tanya asked.

"The Hat Man," Shannon said. "Tall. Wears a hat, like a soft, felt hat from the early part of the twentieth century. No one knows exactly who he is, but lots of people see him. End of the hallways, corners of rooms. He doesn't speak. He just watches."

"The Hat Man," Sue repeated. "We've heard that before."

"Menlo Lab," Ellen said, trying to piece it all together. "But why?"

"A lot of people see him during sleep paralysis," Shannon informed them. "I'm talking all across the globe. We're not sure if he's the same guy, but who knows?"

Shannon turned down a hallway with smaller rooms. "These rooms were for quiet time, like when a patient needed a time out. Down the next corridor, you'll find procedure rooms."

"What kind of procedures?" Tanya wanted to know.

"Experimental. Electroshock therapy, hydrotherapy, insulin shock therapy, lobotomies. They were looking for ways to shock the psychosis from the patients."

"Insulin therapy?" Ellen repeated.

"To put them in comas," Shannon explained.

"It's like the Gold House," Sue commented. Then, to Shannon, she added, "That was our first case."

"You ever walk into a place and feel like it's studying you?" Shannon asked. "That's what the Eloise is like. She watches. She waits. Especially if you're sensitive."

Ellen felt it, too. The low hum in the walls. The tickle at the back of her neck. The faint, unmistakable feeling of *presence*—and *not* the groups in the basement escape rooms.

"Remember, this place first opened in 1839," Shannon said. "That's pre-Civil War. And if a man got tired of his wife, he could leave her here. There weren't doctors back then to confirm whether someone was mentally ill."

"Also like the Gold House," Sue said with a shudder.

"If you think about it," Shannon continued, "A lot of people came here to die. It was the poor house, the insane asylum, and a general hospital, and there was a tuberculosis ward. At one time, there were as many as ten thousand inmates here. Men, women, and children."

"Inmates?" Tanya echoed.

"That what they called them," Shannon explained. "And there's a potter's field across the street where over 7,000 of them were buried between 1910 and 1938 with unmarked graves."

Ellen shivered.

In a back room, they found tiled walls, rusted hooks, and a battered clawfoot tub.

"Hydrotherapy room," Shannon said. "Used for calming agitated patients. There were four of them in the building. The inmates were restrained in lukewarm water for hours, sometimes days."

"Sounds more like torture," Tanya said.

Shannon nodded. "It was, in many cases. They used to experiment with different temperatures—ice cold, scalding hot. Like I said, they wanted to see what might shock the psychosis out of them. And energy like that sticks around."

As if in answer, a slow drip echoed in the silence—except that the faucet and tub were dry.

Sue pointed toward the wall. "There's writing."

A phrase, barely legible in the flaking tile grout: *Don't let him in.*

Shannon glanced around. "That wasn't here when I came in earlier."

They stood in silence.

"Are you sure?" Ellen asked.

Shannon shook her head. "No. That's new."

Tanya cocked her head to the side. "I'm getting a strange feeling, like maybe that has something to do with Charles McElvaine."

"Who's that?" Shannon asked.

"One of the first men—a kid, really—to die by electric chair," Tanya explained. "We think his ghost might be connected with the phenomena occurring at Greenfield Village."

"Hmm. I don't know," Shannon admitted. "We do have a Tesla coil in the basement, but I'm not sure if that's related to your ghost."

They looped around to a narrow corridor, one Shannon referred to as "the echo hall." The walls narrowed, and sound behaved strangely. Footsteps repeated twice. Breaths came back as whispers.

"People report full-body apparitions down here," Shannon said. "Sometimes you hear humming. Sometimes crying."

As they passed a sagging bench near a broken window, Ellen stopped cold.

A shadow stood at the far end of the hallway.

Tall. Unmoving. Wearing a hat.

"Do you see him?" she whispered.

Shannon followed her gaze. "Yep. He's back."

"No way," Tanya whispered, turning as white as a sheet.

The figure didn't move, didn't acknowledge them—but somehow Ellen felt seen. Not just observed. *Known.*

Their flashlights flickered.

Then—just like that—he was gone.

Shannon exhaled slowly. "He doesn't usually show himself that clearly."

Sue crossed her arms. "Could be he's curious. I wonder if he was a patient."

Ellen's mind raced. The Hat Man. The light flickers. Edison—or someone claiming to be Edison—in their sessions. And now *this.*

"Shannon," she said, her voice steady. "Who wired this place? Originally, I mean. Who installed the electrical systems for all of the Eloise?"

Shannon tilted her head. "Detroit Electric."

Ellen sighed and shrugged. "I was sure you were going to say Thomas Edison."

Shannon smiled. "Detroit Electric *was* Thomas Edison. His company wired the asylum. All 78 buildings. His people even converted the original gas plant to electric. You're standing in Edison's footprint."

The temperature seemed to drop. Ellen turned to look at her friends. Tanya's eyes were wide, and Sue was already nodding.

"I think this place is somehow connected to what's happening at the Farris Windmill," Ellen said quietly.

Tanya clicked her tongue. "I was just thinking the same thing. But how?"

Sue put her hands on her hips. "That's what we need to find out."

Shannon took them through the other three floors, where they saw more of the same. "The higher you go, the more intense the paranormal activity is." She explained that women and children lived on the third floor, men on the fourth, and the criminally insane on the fifth. But Ellen barely heard what their guide was saying because her mind was reeling. Could Thomas Edison be connected to this haunted place?

As they made their way back toward the main door, the silence felt heavier—not oppressive, more like an unspoken agreement had been made. Something had been acknowledged, and whatever was watching had let them go, for now.

Shannon held the door open for them, her flashlight glinting off the rusted hinges.

"I can't tell you what's haunting the windmill," she said as they stepped outside, "but I *can* tell you this: places like this don't forget."

C.W. was waiting, sipping from a Styrofoam cup in the idling SUV.

"Well?" he asked, eyes twinkling. "Any spirits say hi?"

Ellen looked back at the towering asylum behind them, now bathed in deepening shadow.

"Oh yeah," she said. "One of them even wore a hat."

Sue turned to Shannon, who was standing on the curb in front of the building. "Do you think it would be possible for us to conduct our own investigation here tonight?"

Shannon frowned. "We have escape room adventures all night on Saturdays, but I could get you in tomorrow night. Our last adventure ends at five tomorrow. There's usually a fee, though."

"That's no problem," Ellen chimed in. "I'm sure John Coleman will pay it."

"Want to come tomorrow night?" Shannon asked. "Say, eight o'clock?"

"It's a date," Sue said with a grin. "See you then."

Once they'd climbed into C.W.'s SUV, Ellen leaned forward. "Could you drive us to the Henry Ford before taking us back to the inn?"

"Why?" Tanya asked from the front passenger's seat.

"I want to see the test tube of Edison's last breath. Do you mind?"

"I don't," Tanya replied. "What about you, Sue?"

"Let's go," she said. "Is that okay, C.W.?"

"Of course. It's not that far from here."

At the museum, they used the badges John had loaned them to get inside, where a petite docent about their age greeted them.

"Hello, I'm Edwardina. Welcome to the Henry Ford. You ladies look like you're on a mission."

"Actually, we are," Ellen replied. "Can you point us in the direction of Edison's last breath?"

"I'll do better. I'll take you there myself. Follow me."

They followed the petite woman past the Model Ts and presidential vehicles to an encased display with a bust of Edison beside a glass test tube. Next to the tube was a card with these words: "Thomas Edison was Henry Ford's hero, as well as his friend. During Edison's final illness, a rack of test tubes was close to his bedside. Upon his death, Edison's son Charles had them sealed with paraffin wax. He sent one to Henry Ford, knowing their close relationship."

Sue tapped Ellen on the shoulder. "Look."

To the right of the bust on another table sat a pair of tan shoes and a black hat that belonged to Edison.

"That hat!" Tanya whispered.

"It's like the one the shadow man was wearing," Ellen said.

The friends thanked Edwardina and hurried back outside to the white SUV, where C.W. was waiting for them.

When they told him about the Hat Man and what they discovered in the museum, C.W. covered his mouth with both hands.

"This is getting crazy," he said.

"Welcome to our world," Sue said from the back seat.

CHAPTER FOURTEEN

Belle Isle

The creak of the front steps echoed behind Ellen as she pulled the door closed against the chilly spring air. The porch light flickered once, then held steady, softly illuminating the decorative welcome mat.

Inside, Ellen dropped her bag on the antique sofa, where Tanya was already curled up with her phone. Sue was in the kitchen, clinking around in the cupboards for plates.

Ellen tugged off her boots and stretched her legs. Her thighs still ached from all the walking they'd done around the Eastern Market. And then there'd been the Eloise—cold floors, tight hallways, and the haunting image of the Hat Man burned into her brain.

Now, though, with the promise of pizza on the way and good Wi-Fi, she was determined to dig deeper.

"So," Tanya said, eyes fixed on her screen, "I started looking into Charles McElvaine. Not a lot to go on, but I'm finding breadcrumbs."

Ellen grabbed her laptop from her bag and settled next to her. "What've you got so far?"

"Early 1900s," Tanya said. "He was nineteen, executed by electric chair at the Sing Sing Correctional Facility in New York, and was the only one on record to be executed using Edison's controversial method—hand-to-hand current instead of the usual head-to-leg setup."

"That checks with what we read earlier," Sue called from the kitchen.

"Edison was testing a theory," Tanya muttered. "Or making a statement. The whole war between Edison and Westinghouse was brutal. And this kid might've been a pawn."

Ellen opened a tab and typed "Charles McElvaine" into Google. Most of the results were historical footnotes or brief mentions in books about capital punishment or the evolution of electricity. No Wikipedia page. No photo.

"No family?" she asked.

"I found a marriage record," Tanya said. "He was married at age seventeen and was arrested six months later."

"What was the crime? Murder, right?" Sue asked, coming into the room with three mismatched plates and setting them on the coffee table.

"Robbery and accomplice to murder," Ellen said, scanning one of the old newspaper clippings. "He and a friend tried to rob a grocer. The friend shot the man. Charles ran but was caught. His friend got away."

"He didn't pull the trigger?" Sue asked.

"No," Ellen said softly. "But he was convicted as an accomplice. There was a lot of pressure to make an example. The papers called it 'the crime of the new century.' Poor thing was only seventeen at the time and was executed two years later."

"He truly was a kid," Tanya said.

Sue sat down with a groan. "So, Edison wanted to use this execution to show up the doctors—and poor Charles got turned into a science project."

Ellen kept reading. A boy from Brooklyn. Only child. Parents dead by the time he was sixteen. Married young to a woman named Lillian Beatrice Keller.

"Listen to this," she said, reading aloud: "'Mrs. Lillian McElvaine wept silently throughout the sentencing, refusing to leave the courtroom until she had touched her husband's hand one last time.'"

"That's heartbreaking," Tanya murmured.

"Wait," Ellen said, clicking another link. "There's a letter."

"A letter?" Sue leaned in.

"Apparently Charles wrote to the governor of New York from prison. Someone transcribed it. It's short, but…"

She cleared her throat and read aloud:

To His Excellency, Governor Hill,

I am writing to beg for my life. I understand the weight of what I did. But I ask that you understand I did not intend to cause harm. I was afraid. I followed a friend into darkness, out of desperation. Please reconsider my sentence. My fate is in your hands.

Yours in regret,

Charles E. McElvaine

The room was silent.

"God," Sue finally whispered. "How sad."

Ellen closed her laptop slowly, the words echoing in her mind. A seventeen-year-old boy, poor and orphaned, pulled into something terrible by the wrong person at the wrong time. Heck, they were robbing a grocer. The articles didn't say whether they were stealing money or food. Nevertheless, he was then sacrificed—not just for his crime, but for Edison's agenda.

"He's stuck," Ellen said.

Tanya looked up. "You think he's the spirit at the windmill?"

"I think he's *connected* somehow. Whether he's there or just part of what's bleeding through, I don't know. But if that windmill's tied to Edison—and the Eloise was wired by Edison's people—and Charles was Edison's first and only hand-to-hand execution—there's a pattern forming."

Sue sipped her Cherry Coke. "Maybe we're not just chasing ghosts. Maybe we're unraveling a network."

Ellen stood and walked to the bay window. Outside, the glow of the Dearborn Inn's carriage lamps flickered through the trees. The road was quiet. The wind rustled the early spring leaves like whispered voices.

"Imagine dying like that," Ellen said softly. "Alone, misunderstood. Your body used in an experiment—and then forgotten."

"Well," Tanya said, looking up from her phone, "not anymore. We remember him now."

A knock came at the door, causing all three ladies to jump in their seats.

"Pizza!" Sue cried, scrambling up like a teenager on movie night.

Ellen smiled despite herself. As Sue opened the door and paid the delivery guy, the scent of garlic, tomato, and melted cheese drifted into the room like a benediction.

They gathered around the coffee table, the heaviness of the evening softened by mozzarella and marinara.

But as Ellen took her first bite, her thoughts drifted back to Charles. Not the crime. Not the chair.

But the way he had signed his name.

Yours in regret.

A boy who'd stepped into darkness and never found his way back.

Maybe it was time someone lit the path.

Sunday morning unfolded with a gentle golden hue over the Patrick Henry House.

Tanya entered the sitting room and retrieved her jacket from the hook by the front door. "C.W. will be here in ten minutes."

Sue sat down to put on her boots. "Tell him I'll buy him a coffee if he detours us past a bakery. I need a maple-glazed donut or I might die."

"What happened to needing only one meal a day?" Ellen asked with a chuckle as she strapped on her cross-body purse.

"That's only when I'm at the casino," Sue replied.

Ellen stepped out onto the front porch and surveyed the sky, glad to see that the silver dome and constant drizzle had dispersed. "Looks like it's going to be a beautiful day."

"Oh goodie," Sue, joining her, said. Then she sang, "These boots are made for walkin', and that's just what they'll do."

"Someone's in a good mood," Ellen said with a grin.

"I was looking up real estate in Branson last night, and I found the perfect place," Sue explained. "I was so excited I couldn't sleep— hence my need for coffee and sugar."

"Tell us about it," Tanya prompted as she joined them on the porch.

"It's a fixer-upper on a big piece of land. There are even stories about buried treasure."

"How fun," Ellen exclaimed. "I hope the plan is for the three of us to renovate."

"Of course!" Sue said. "But first, I need to convince Tom."

"Then you better start being nice to him," Tanya warned.

"I'm always nice."

"There's C.W.," Ellen pointed out as the white SUV pulled up to the curb. "Right on time."

"Good morning, ladies," he said, opening the doors for them. "Per Sue's request, I picked up coffee and donuts from Dutch Girl. Hope you're hungry."

"You're the best, C.W.," Sue beamed, accepting a cup of coffee.

As they settled into the vehicle, the aroma of donuts filled the air, setting a cheerful tone for the day.

The drive to Belle Isle was serene, the city gradually giving way to the lush greenery of the island park. Their first stop was the Anna Scripps Whitcomb Conservatory. The historic greenhouse, with its majestic dome, stood as a testament to Detroit's rich botanical heritage. The ladies invited C.W. to join them.

"No reason to wait in the car," Sue pointed out. "If you're interested, that is."

Inside, they were enveloped by a world of vibrant flora. The Palm House soared above them, housing towering tropical trees. The Orchid Room showcased delicate blooms in a myriad of colors, each more enchanting than the last. Ellen found herself drawn to a particular orchid, its petals a deep violet with specks of gold.

"It's called the 'Midnight Star,'" a conservatory guide explained. He was a young man, early twenties, with light brown curls and a short beard. "Rare and known for its unique coloration."

"It's lovely," Ellen said. "I've never seen so many orchids."

"We have the largest collection in the world," the young man informed her.

Sue and Tanya caught up to them.

"I think my clematis needs an orchid to keep it company," Tanya said.

"Unfortunately, these aren't for sale," the guide informed her.

"I wouldn't have room on the plane anyway," Tanya admitted. "I'm just dreaming."

"If you need a list of recommendations, let me know," the guide offered before heading down another aisle with his watering can.

Next, they visited the Belle Isle Aquarium. The historic building, with its green-tiled, arched ceiling, evoked an underwater ambiance. They marveled at the diverse aquatic life, from vibrant coral reefs to mysterious deep-sea creatures. Sue was particularly fascinated by the electric eel exhibit.

"Nature's own electrical engineer," Sue mused.

C.W. chuckled. "Reminds me of our friend, Edison."

Ellen smiled, the connection not lost on her.

Their journey continued to the Belle Isle Nature Center. Here, they encountered native reptiles, amphibians, and an observation hive buzzing with honeybees. Tanya was enthralled by the interactive exhibits, while Ellen appreciated the center's dedication to environmental education.

They took a leisurely stroll through the surrounding trails, the sounds of nature providing a soothing backdrop.

Curiosity led them to the Dossin Great Lakes Museum. The maritime exhibits offered a glimpse into Detroit's nautical history. They admired the collection of model ships and the anchor of the *SS Edmund Fitzgerald.*

Ellen stood before a display detailing the evolution of maritime navigation. "It's fascinating how technology has transformed over the years," she remarked.

C.W. nodded. "From compasses to GPS, yet the essence of exploration remains unchanged."

As the afternoon sun began its descent, they made their way to Sindbad's Restaurant and Marina. The waterfront eatery, established in 1949, offered panoramic views of the Detroit River. They chose a table on the patio, the gentle breeze complementing the ambiance.

Over plates of fresh fish, shrimp, and Angus beef sirloin steaks, they engaged in heartfelt conversation.

"C.W., you've been our guide and friend throughout this journey," Ellen began. "Tell us more about yourself."

He smiled, taking a sip of his drink. "Well, I'm descended from the great Ojibwe, born right here in Detroit. Spent some years in Chicago before returning to start a family. My wife passed away a few years ago, but my son and daughter-in-law have blessed me with grandchildren who keep me on my toes. I taught photography for many years at various schools—both high school and college—before retiring."

"I always wanted to learn photography," Tanya said, before taking a sip of her hot tea.

"I also serve as a deacon at the Basilica of Sainte Anne once a month," he added.

Sue raised her glass, "To C.W., a man of many hats."

Ellen shivered, recalling the Hat Man, as she lifted her glass.

They clinked glasses, bringing a smile to C.W.'s face.

As dusk settled, they returned to the Patrick Henry House. While C.W. waited in the car, the trio gathered their equipment, along with a sage smudge stick for protection. Their mission was clear—to speak with the spirits of Charles McElvaine and Thomas Edison and to discover how they connected with the whispering windmill.

C.W. sat patiently behind the wheel, the SUV waiting for their next adventure.

"Ready, ladies?" he called out.

"Always," Sue said before climbing into the back with Ellen.

"As ready as I'll ever be," Tanya said with a half-smile.

CHAPTER FIFTEEN

The Hat Man

The Uber crept away into the night like a ghost, its red tail lights fading into the blackness beyond the cracked pavement of Michigan Avenue. A low fog slithered over the overgrown lawn, curling around the broken sign that read *Eloise Psychiatric Hospital.* Ellen tugged her coat more tightly around her as she stepped forward, flanked by Sue and Tanya, each of them silent as they stared up at the sprawling, decaying structure.

C.W. had dropped them off with a wave and a good-luck-you'll-need-it grin before peeling off into the darkness. That was ten seconds ago. Already, it felt like an hour.

The Eloise loomed above them, its brick façade covered in soot and ivy, windows like black, empty eyes. Most were boarded up, but a few were cracked, shattered, or gaping open, like mouths ready to whisper secrets. A cool breeze swept through the broken glass and echoed down the hallways inside.

Ellen heard it whisper her name. Or maybe it was just the wind.

Shannon, their tour guide from the previous afternoon, was waiting at the side entrance. She was dressed in black jeans and a leather jacket and was holding a clipboard. A flashlight dangled from her wrist.

"You're right on time," Shannon said with a smile that didn't quite reach her eyes. "Just sign the waiver, and we're all set. You've got the place until 1 a.m. No one else booked tonight. Enjoy."

They signed quickly. Tanya handed over the envelope of cash. Shannon tucked it into her jacket, then handed over the key.

"Make sure you lock up behind you when you go in," she warned, "and behind you when you leave. Drop the key in that drop box." She pointed to a stone structure resembling a mailbox. "And good luck. If anything gets too real, just remember, you chose to come here, and you can leave whenever you want."

She gave a little wave and walked off briskly toward the lot.

And just like that, they were alone at the asylum.

After she unlocked the door and let the three of them inside, Ellen took a deep breath, locked the door behind them, and slid the key into her coat pocket. Headlamps clicked on one by one, making circles of light in the darkness. Their boots echoed down the long corridor as they made their way to the stairwell.

"I still can't believe we saw him here in daylight," Tanya whispered, her voice reverent. "The Hat Man."

Ellen nodded but said nothing. She was already clutching the SLS camera in her right hand and a spirit box in her left. Their destination was the second floor—where, just the day before, they'd caught the shadowy figure of a tall man wearing a hat peering at them from the end of the corridor.

Now, they were back. At night.

The second-floor hallway felt colder. Ellen's breath fogged in front of her. They passed peeling murals on the walls—flowers, children's drawings, suns and moons—all faded and cracked like the memories of the people who once lived here.

They stepped into the rec room.

It was larger than Ellen remembered. At the center sat the old dentist's chair, its cracked leather seat tilted like an invitation. Against the far wall, a battered billiards table was folded on its side. A rusted treadmill leaned drunkenly in one corner, and near it stood a squat, old-fashioned television cart.

"Okay, team," Ellen said softly. "Let's get this set up."

They moved with quiet precision, having now performed these acts dozens of times. Sue lit three candles and placed them in the center of the room, the flames flickering against the grime-streaked windows. Tanya set up the first full-spectrum camera in the far-right corner. Ellen mounted the second facing the chair, and Sue positioned the third near the entrance.

Ellen then placed a Mini Maglite on the floor near the treadmill, unscrewing the cap just enough so a spirit could turn it on or off by touch. Across the room, she set up a REM-Pod, its red light flaring to life in the dark.

Sue lit her sage smudge stick. The smoke curled in soft tendrils, spiraling toward the ceiling.

"Spirits of this place," Sue intoned, sweeping the sage in a circle around them, "we come in peace. No harm, no fear. We ask that any negative energies leave this room now."

The smoke stung Ellen's eyes, but she welcomed it. Rituals like this mattered, even if only to calm their own nerves.

Sue raised her voice just slightly. "To those spirits who mean no harm, who seek peace—we are here to listen. We want to hear your story. We want to help."

Ellen powered on the spirit box, the static hissing in her hand. She braced herself for nothing, but there was something, loud and clear.

"Hello," a child's voice crackled through the white noise.

They all froze.

Sue leaned closer. "Hello. Who is this?"

"Patricia," the voice answered, faint but clear. "I'm ten years old."

Ellen met Tanya's wide eyes, then looked to Sue, who was smiling despite the chill in the air.

"Hello, Patricia," Ellen said, steadying her voice. "Are you here alone? Or are there others with you?"

There was a pause. Then:

"Come upstairs."

Sue lifted her brows. "Should we?"

Ellen nodded. "We may as well. Let's see where this goes."

Sue grabbed a full-spectrum camera from its tripod, and together, they made their way up the staircase, the echo of their boots bouncing back at them in waves. The third floor was even colder. Shadows clustered in the corners like waiting things. Their headlamps cut through the darkness.

"This looks like one of the sleeping wards," Tanya murmured. "Wasn't this the women and children's floor?"

"I think you're right," Sue said.

Rows of metal bed frames, stripped of mattresses, were scattered across the floor. Broken blinds hung from the windows. Graffiti covered the walls—some of it childish, some of it cruel.

"Come to the mirror," said the spirit box.

They scanned the room. No mirrors.

"There may have been a mirror here when Patricia was alive," Ellen offered.

"Over here," the box urged.

Sue's EMF detector started to squeal. She turned in a slow circle, following the beeping toward the hall. "This way."

They followed the signal down the corridor until Tanya stopped short. "That room—there's a mirror."

They slipped into the small chamber.

White tile covered the walls. A rusty drain in the middle of the floor glinted beneath their lights. The mirror, smeared and cracked, was bolted to the far wall.

"This was probably another hydrotherapy room," Ellen muttered. "Shannon said there were four in the building."

"I don't see anything in the mirror," Sue said, stepping forward.

"Let's try turning off our headlamps," Ellen suggested. "Use the camera's infrared."

Click.

The darkness closed in like a curtain.

Ellen's breath caught.

There, in the mirror, stood five children staring back at them.

"Oh, my God," Tanya whispered.

Ellen turned, her heart hammering. There was no one behind them, but in the mirror, the children remained.

Tears welled in her eyes, and she stood frozen in fear.

Sue's voice trembled. "Hi there. Is one of you Patricia?"

The mirror clouded, then emptied. The children were gone.

"Stay away from the Hat Man," warned the spirit box.

Tanya stared at the device. "Are you trying to protect us?"

"Fearful," the box replied. "Run."

Ellen looked at her friends. Tanya's hands shook. Sue's lips pressed into a line.

"Do they want us to leave?" Tanya asked.

"Get out," came the reply.

Ellen bit her lip. "But the Hat Man is the very thing we need to talk to."

Sue hesitated, then nodded. "Let's go back downstairs."

They moved quickly now, the adrenaline rushing through them. The third floor felt like it was pushing them out. The second floor swallowed them back up.

The rec room was unchanged. The dentist's chair sat waiting. The candles had burned lower, the wax pooled into teardrops.

Sue placed the full-spectrum camera back on its tripod, and Ellen reset the REM-Pod. It whined to life.

Tanya replaced her headphones and held up the EVP recorder.

The spirit box whispered.

And somewhere—far down the hall—a slow, deliberate footstep echoed.

They all froze.

Then, another step.

Ellen strained her ears, her headlamp now a dull circle against the faded walls of the rec room. The air had thickened, heavier than the sage smoke curling faintly in the corners. Her fingers pressed more tightly around the SLS camera, its screen still showing nothing.

The dentist's chair creaked as though settling under invisible weight.

The REM-Pod beeped, causing all three women to jump.

Then the spirit box crackled.

"It's me."

Ellen blinked at the device, then leaned closer. "Who's *me?*"

There was a pause, the white noise intensifying.

"Al."

Ellen's spine stiffened. "Al?" she echoed. Her brain jumped to the only possibility that made sense—one they'd all been circling since the moment the Hat Man had first appeared.

"Thomas *Alva* Edison?" Sue asked.

The spirit box responded in a voice that was calm and exact. "Precisely."

For a heartbeat, no one spoke. Even the air seemed to hold its breath.

"Why are you here?" Sue asked carefully, her voice quieter now, reverent almost, as though they were in a cathedral instead of a crumbling hospital for the forgotten.

"Many reasons," the box replied.

Ellen steadied the SLS camera, scanning toward the hallway, the screen still void of any stick figures. "Can you tell us one of them?"

The answer came fast.

"Experiments."

Tanya frowned. "What kind of experiments?"

"On the . . . dead."

Ellen's breath caught.

"What kind of experiments?" Sue pressed.

"Scientific."

Ellen sighed, low and frustrated. "That's not helpful."

A flicker of motion in the corner of the room caught her attention, but when she turned, there was nothing. Still, her skin prickled.

She pointed the SLS camera at the corner and picked up on a human-like figure.

"The camera's picking up on him," Ellen whispered.

"Can you tell us *another* reason why you're here?" Sue asked, keeping her voice even.

There was a pause.

Then: "Atonement."

The word hung in the room like a chill.

Ellen turned her head slowly to look at Sue and Tanya. All three of them had widened eyes, their bodies frozen in place as though bracing for what came next.

"Why atonement?" Ellen asked, gazing at the screen on her camera and the movement of the stick-figure moving toward her.

"You know."

The tone was different now. A little deeper. Not threatening, exactly, but heavy with implication.

Tanya adjusted her headphones slightly, her EVP recorder still rolling. "The electric chair?" she asked, as if already suspecting the answer.

"Yes."

Ellen's throat went dry as she took a step back. They'd done their research—how Edison had thrown his weight behind alternating current's dangers during the "War of Currents," how he'd championed the electric chair not just as a method of humane execution but as a public smear campaign against his rivals, Westinghouse and Tesla. The legacy was complicated.

But hearing *him* say it?

That was something else.

She drew a breath. "Is Charles McElvaine here with you?"

"No. The lab."

"Menlo Lab?" Sue asked, her voice steady now.

"Exactly."

The three women stood in tense silence, absorbing the implications.

Charles McElvaine, the nineteen-year-old guinea pig in Edison's experimental electric chair, was not here.

Not in this building.

But at Edison's old laboratory?

Ellen's thoughts spun. She gripped the spirit box tighter. "Is Charles McElvaine the darkness? Is *he* evil?"

There was a longer pause this time.

"No."

Another heartbeat passed.

"I am."

The sentence landed like a weight in the center of the room. All the warmth from the candles seemed to snuff out, even though their flames still flickered.

Tanya's voice cracked, barely above a whisper. "Oh, my God."

The REM-Pod flared to life in the corner near the stick figure, beeping frantically for two seconds, then went silent as the stick figure on her camera disappeared.

In the doorway, something moved.

As she turned, Ellen's headlamp caught the faintest shimmer of a tall figure—black coat, black hat, indistinct and flickering like a projection caught in static. The shadow stood still for only a second, but long enough for her to see two distinct red eyes beneath the brim of the hat.

Then the figure turned and vanished into the corridor.

Ellen let out a shaky breath. "Oh, my gosh. That was him again."

"Thomas Edison *is* the darkness," Tanya whispered. Her hands trembled as she lowered her headphones.

"What do we do now?" Ellen asked, even though she already felt the answer in her bones.

"We need to talk to Charles McElvaine," Sue said. "Tomorrow. At Menlo Lab."

Ellen gave a slow nod, trying to still her pounding heart. "Agreed."

They moved fast after that.

Packing their instruments felt like a ritual of reassurance—SLS camera zipped up, batteries secured, full-spectrum cameras detached from tripods and zipped into their padded bags. Sue blew out the candles, one by one. Tanya turned off the EVP recorder and double-checked her files.

Ellen cast one last glance at the dentist's chair.

Still empty.

Still waiting.

They walked briskly down the corridor, their headlamps bouncing off peeling wallpaper and dust-covered plaques. They made their way down the narrow stairs. The atmosphere shifted with each step they took toward the exit, like the building itself was loosening its grip on them.

By the time they reached the side entrance and stepped out into the night, the air felt different.

Cold, but clean.

Tanya was already pulling out her phone and texting C.W. as Ellen locked the door behind them.

Ellen put the key in the mail drop near the exit. Then, she caught up to Sue and Tanya near the edge of the cracked sidewalk, facing the hulking asylum. The building loomed behind them, its dark windows gleaming faintly beneath the moonlight.

"Don't follow us home," Ellen whispered, not even sure to whom she spoke—Edison, the Hat Man, or whatever else lived inside those walls. Maybe all of them. "Please, stay here."

Sue came up beside her, placing a steadying hand on Ellen's shoulder.

"You okay?" she asked.

Ellen nodded. "I think so. Just processing."

Their Uber driver pulled up a few minutes later, headlights slicing through the mist.

C.W. leaned out the window, grinning. "Y'all still in one piece?"

"Barely," Tanya muttered as she opened the front passenger's door.

They piled in, the warmth of the vehicle wrapping around them like a soft blanket. As C.W. pulled away, Ellen looked back through the rear window. The asylum shrank into the night behind them, but the weight of what had happened inside still clung to her.

In the silence of the ride, she thought about Edison.

Not just the genius inventor—the image taught in schools—but the man who had chosen fear as a tool. Who had twisted science into spectacle. He now wandered the shadows, not as a hero, but as a ghost burdened by atonement.

He'd said *he* was the darkness.

And Ellen believed him.

When they arrived at the Patrick Henry House, the lights inside were still on, spilling a yellow glow across the lawn. Comforting. Human. The house had its own ghosts, of course, but tonight, Ellen welcomed the familiar.

She turned to Sue and Tanya as they stepped out of the car. "Let's get some sleep. Tomorrow, we go to Menlo."

And tomorrow, she would call out to the ghost of Charles McElvaine and try to unravel the rest of the mystery.

But tonight, she would keep the lights on and maybe say another prayer that the shadow with the hat stayed where he belonged.

CHAPTER SIXTEEN

Trigger Object

Ellen wrapped her hands around her steaming mug, savoring the rich scent of freshly brewed coffee as it mingled with the faint tang of leftover sage still clinging to her sweater. The sitting room at the Patrick Henry House was cozy that Monday morning, sunlight slipping through gauzy curtains and casting golden streaks across the hardwood floor. A pink bakery box sat open on the coffee table, revealing a half-eaten maple bar, two chocolate frosted donuts, and what remained of a bear claw that looked like it had lost a fight.

Sue plopped onto the couch beside her, clutching her own mug and eyeing the box with strategic intent. "I call dibs on the chocolate one. Unless Tanya's feeling mean."

"I already had two," Tanya said, reclining in the wingback chair across from them with her feet curled under her. "I'm trying not to die today."

"Oh, goodie." Sue swooped in and claimed the donut like a victorious seagull, then took a generous bite before groaning with pleasure. "Ugh, I needed this."

Ellen smiled and sipped her coffee, letting the familiar comfort of her friends' banter work its healing magic. After the events of last night—the voices, the mirror children, the Hat Man—they'd all agreed a slow morning was essential. No ghost hunting, no history books. Just donuts and decompression.

Sue dabbed her mouth with a napkin, then said around another bite, "So, I think C.W. likes me."

Tanya arched an eyebrow. Ellen nearly snorted coffee from her nose.

Sue held up a hand. "No, I'm serious! Did you see the way he looked at me when I tripped over that curb last night? Concerned. Tender."

"He was probably wondering if you needed a medic," Ellen said, laughing. "Or an exorcist."

"No, no, no." Sue wagged her finger. "There was a definite twinkle. And I caught him smiling when I told him about Mo Mummy. That's basically flirting."

Ellen leaned back and smirked. "Mo Mummy better watch out. There's a new man in town."

They all burst into laughter.

Sue tossed a throw pillow at Ellen. "I'm just saying, the man is *chivalrous*. Opens doors. Drives with two hands. Calls us 'ladies.'"

"That's a high bar," Ellen teased.

"He also volunteers at his church and probably files his taxes early," Tanya added.

"Don't tempt me," Sue said dramatically. "If Tom won't accept my new relationship with the casino, maybe a new man will."

Ellen grinned, then noticed Tanya had gone quiet. Sue noticed too and turned her head.

"You haven't said how things are with Dave," Sue said gently. "On our last trip, you felt like the two of you were living separate lives. Has anything changed?"

Tanya took a long sip of her coffee before answering. "Somewhat. I've accepted we're in a new phase. We spend less time together than we used to, but he's making an effort. He comes up for air from his work more often now. Invites me out for lunch. A walk in the park. Little things."

"That's good to hear," Sue said warmly. "And you spent last Christmas at the house in Biloxi. How did that go?"

"It was nice. I mean, he did take his laptop and answer work calls while we were there, but it was still nice, especially with Mike and Camie there with us."

"That really does sound nice," Ellen said.

Tanya nodded. "It was. I think we're both figuring out how to be together when we're no longer the same people we were at thirty. And that's okay, though sometimes I feel like I hardly know him."

"Knowing him isn't always better," Sue said with a mischievous grin. "Sometimes I wish I knew less about Tom."

Ellen chuckled. Sue could always be counted on to lighten the mood.

"Good point," Tanya conceded.

Sue turned to her. "Everything still good in the McManius household?"

Ellen's smile deepened. "Yeah. It took Brian and me some time to figure each other out, especially that first year or two. Thank goodness for the art studio in Santa Fe."

"We need to go back there again soon," Tanya put in.

Ellen continued, "Brian and I came with a lot of baggage—me more than him—but we've found a rhythm."

"Must be nice," Sue said wistfully, taking another bite of her donut. "I'm not sure if Tom and I ever had a rhythm—though he couldn't snap his fingers to the beat if his life depended on it."

Ellen chuckled. "Have things calmed down between you two? Or is he still mad about the gambling?"

Sue shrugged and held up her hands. "Well, I don't think he wants to kill me anymore, so that's an improvement."

Tanya laughed. "That's our bar now?"

Sue grinned wickedly. "Look, maybe I should just give up on him and run away with C.W. I noticed we passed a couple of casinos on our way to Belle Isle yesterday. Maybe I can tempt him."

Ellen and Tanya groaned and laughed, shaking their heads.

"Or," Tanya said, wiping a tear from the corner of her eye, "you could expedite the sale of the Montana house and get Tom to agree to the one in Branson. New house, no more gambling, happy marriage."

Sue gave her a mock frown. "I guess that depends on how C.W. feels about gambling."

Ellen cocked her head thoughtfully. "Somehow, I think a deacon for the Catholic Church might not encourage your obsession with Mo Mummy and slot machines."

Sue sighed dramatically. "You may have a point there. I guess I'm stuck with Tom."

They all laughed again, the kind of laugh that made the whole room warmer. Outside, the trees swayed gently, their leaves beginning to thaw.

Late Monday morning, under a brightening March sky, Ellen stood on the porch of the Patrick Henry House with Sue and Tanya, their breath still visible but thinner than in days past. The chill had given way to a teasing warmth, promising the onset of spring. As they waited, each of them hoisted a padded bag laden with their ghost-hunting equipment.

John Coleman pulled up in his black Ford Explorer precisely at eleven, the vehicle's engine purring as he rolled down the window.

"Morning, ladies," he called with a cheerful nod. "Menlo Lab, right?"

"Right as rain," Sue said, opening the back door. "And hopefully a little warmer than yesterday."

Tanya climbed into the front seat while Ellen and Sue slid into the back. As they drove down Michigan Avenue toward Greenfield Village, Ellen saw more Canadian geese along the roadside.

"Thanks again for the ride, John," Tanya said as they arrived at the Menlo Lab.

"Well, it's I who should thank you," he said. "And I don't think I've done that enough."

"We'll call you when we're ready," Ellen promised.

Ellen led the way up the steps of Menlo Lab, shouldering open the door. The familiar musty air greeted them, tinged with old wood, wax, and something faintly electric. Dust motes spiraled in the sunbeams cutting through the tall windows. Inside, the reconstructed lab stood preserved in time: wood benches, coil machines, dangling wires, dusty jars, and at the center, the reconstructed phonograph.

"Let's hope it doesn't start spinning on its own," Tanya muttered as they headed upstairs.

There it was, amid walls lined with jars and beneath lines of incandescent bulbs, the thing they had come to see: Edison's electric chair.

"Still gives me the creeps," Tanya murmured, eyeing the chair.

"That makes two of us," Ellen said.

"Three," Sue added, dropping her bag beside a nearby workbench. "But what can you do? It's why we're here."

They began unpacking their gear. Cameras were mounted, meters calibrated, candles arranged. Sue set the spirit box on the bench closest to the electric chair, her eyes glinting.

They began as always by letting the spirits know that they came in peace and meant no harm. They introduced themselves and called out to Charles McElvaine. But the spirit box was silent save the pulsing of the channels rapidly changing.

"I have an idea," Sue said.

"That usually means trouble," Tanya said warily.

"Oh, hush. Listen. We use the electric chair as a trigger object. Tanya, you sit in the chair."

"Why me?"

"Because you fit. And because ghosts like you."

Tanya gave her a withering look, but Ellen was already nodding. "It makes sense. Charles McElvaine might respond if he thinks history is repeating itself."

Tanya rolled her eyes and sat gingerly in the chair. Sue helped her strap the worn leather cuffs around her wrists and ankles. Ellen attached an electrode to Tanya's head and calf.

"Okay," Sue began, "electrocute the prisoner."

Ellen pretended to push a lever as she asked, "Charles McElvaine, are you here with us?"

Static filled the room, soft and steady. Tanya pretended to spasm.

"Charles," Sue called. "We need answers. Is Edison the shadowy figure we've seen? The one in the hat?"

A few seconds of silence.

Then, broken and whispery: "Yes. Edison. Hat Man."

All three women stiffened.

Sue leaned closer. "Is he evil? Is he the darkness?"

The box crackled. "Yes . . . evil . . . opened . . . portal."

Ellen's heart thudded. She looked at Sue, who mouthed *portal?*

"What kind of portal?" Sue asked.

The answer was slower this time. "Connecting."

Ellen swallowed hard. "Connecting what?"

The voice returned, clearer this time: "The realms."

The Mini Maglite flickered erratically. Two of the candles went out at once, their smoke curling upward. A sudden crash made all three women jump as a glass jar toppled from a shelf and shattered against the wooden floor.

"Bad!" the spirit box snapped.

"What's bad?" Sue asked quickly as Ellen recovered from the crash. "Edison?"

"Portal . . . dangerous . . . bad."

Ellen exhaled slowly. "How is it dangerous?"

The static swelled before another answer emerged: "Destroys . . . life."

All three women gasped.

"Destroys life?" Tanya repeated. "How?"

Ellen felt the hair rise on her arms. "What can we do?"

Another jar crashed to the floor, causing the ladies to jump.

The lights above flickered again.

Then the spirit box hissed, "Controlled."

Ellen repeated, "Controlled?"

The name "Edison" came over the spirit box.

"Edison?" Tanya repeated. "Is Edison controlled?"

"How?" Sue asked.

"Blackmail," the spirit box said.

They turned to each other in stunned silence.

"Someone is blackmailing Edison?" Tanya said slowly. "Into making a portal?"

Ellen snapped her fingers. "The windmill! It's the portal!"

"Yes," the spirit box said.

"Who is controlling Edison?" Sue asked.

The spirit box sputtered, but no words came. Just static.

"Sometimes the radio doesn't give them access to the words they need," Ellen reminded them. "If the name isn't being said on a radio broadcast, they can't use it."

"We need the Ouija board," Sue said, digging into her bag. She laid the board on an old desk and motioned for them to join her. They stood around the board and placed their fingers lightly on the planchette before "opening" the board.

Sue took a breath. "Charles McElvaine, please tell us the name of the person who is blackmailing Edison."

The planchette sat still for a long moment. Then it began to move.

F-L-I-N-T.

"Flint," Ellen whispered. "George Flint. We met him the other day!"

Tanya's eyes widened. "The curator who came when we were with Leroy!"

Sue leaned in. "Charles, how is George Flint blackmailing Thomas Edison?"

The planchette stilled.

Then, over the spirit box: "Secret diary."

"George has a secret diary that belonged to Edison?" Ellen asked.

The planchette slid decisively to YES.

There was a high whine over the spirit box, then an explosive pop of static.

Then: "Close . . . the . . . portal!"

The overhead lights surged and went dark.

The spirit box sputtered and died, drained of its battery.

Another glass jar fell, exploding into shards.

The room plunged into silence.

Ellen, Sue, and Tanya stood frozen around the Ouija board, their fingers still touching the planchette. Their breathing was the only sound.

Tanya whispered, "Did he say *close* the portal?"

"That's what it sounded like," Ellen said, pulse pounding.

"And that George Flint is blackmailing Edison with a secret diary," Sue added.

Ellen took a steadying breath. "Then we need to find that diary and figure out how to close the portal, before life is destroyed."

Sue grimaced. "I guess we now know why the windmill is whispering."

Ellen nodded, trying to process the gravity of their situation: The portal at the windmill destroys life. What did that mean, exactly?

They stood together in the dim, haunted silence of Menlo Lab, the air electric with warnings from the dead and the weight of what they would have to do next.

The Curator

The wind had picked up by the time John Coleman pulled to a stop just outside the Greenfield Village gate. Ellen, Sue, and Tanya piled into his black Ford Explorer, the March breeze still clinging to their jackets and hair. Their equipment bags sagged with the weight of cameras, sensors, and spirit boxes. Tanya slammed the door shut and gave John a grateful smile.

"So," John said, glancing at them in the rearview mirror as he pulled away from the curb, "judging by the looks on your faces, I'm guessing something happened at Menlo Lab."

"Something big," Sue replied, tugging her seatbelt into place. "We made contact—with Charles McElvaine."

John's brow lifted slightly. "The ghost tied to the electric chair?"

"That's the one," Ellen said. She leaned forward between the front seats. "He dropped a major bomb."

John merged onto the access road toward the museum campus. "Which is?"

"That Thomas Edison opened a portal between the living and the dead," Ellen said evenly.

John chuckled. "You're serious."

"*Dead* serious," Sue said with a grin.

Tanya gave Sue a look of disapproval. "It's no joking matter. It's dangerous to the living. McElvaine said Edison was forced to do it. Blackmailed."

"By someone here," Ellen added. "An employee."

"One of *my* employees?" John asked with raised brows.

Tanya nodded. "George Flint."

The car went quiet.

"George Flint?" John repeated. "Our curator?"

Sue leaned forward. "Apparently, he has a secret diary—one written by Edison—containing some kind of damaging confession. McElvaine said Flint used it to coerce Edison into opening the portal at the Farris Windmill."

"Which explains the constant whispering," Tanya added. "And the sightings. The windmill is the portal."

John let out a long breath, one hand tightening around the steering wheel. "That's a hell of an accusation. Do you have proof?"

"Not yet," Ellen admitted. "But I have a theory. If the electric chair and the diary came from the same auction, there must've been an invoice listing all included items. Maybe even some notes about provenance."

John nodded slowly. "That's true."

"So, rather than take us back to the Patrick Henry House," Ellen began sweetly, "would you be willing to check your records?"

Without another word, John turned the wheel and headed for the museum's administrative offices.

On the way, Sue asked, "What can you tell us about George?"

"He's a mild-mannered man and a good employee. Been here for at least ten years, maybe longer. His wife died of cancer last year, and about five years before that, the couple lost their only child—a daughter named Heather. Died of ovarian cancer in her mid-twenties."

"Oh, how sad," Tanya said, articulating what Ellen was thinking.

"That's motive," Sue pointed out.

Ellen sighed. She supposed Sue was right. Losing your wife and an only child might make a man desperate enough to blackmail Edison's ghost into opening a portal, so he could see his wife and daughter again.

"You're right," Tanya said from the front seat.

The building was tucked behind the main visitor complex, a modest brick structure with narrow stairs leading to a second-floor suite of offices. John parked, and the trio followed him up the steps and into a bright, neatly organized workspace with white walls, framed photographs, and the faint scent of copier toner in the air.

John ushered them into his office and gestured for them to sit while he logged into his desktop computer. Ellen perched on the edge of a chair, her heart fluttering with anticipation.

"Give me a sec," John said, typing rapidly. "The electric chair came in last August, as I recall. That was a private sale, I think, not an auction."

Ellen leaned forward. "Do you think George Flint may have kept the diary for himself?"

"I suppose it's possible," John said. "But anything purchased for Greenfield Village should be documented."

They waited in tense silence as John scrolled through his files.

"Here we go," he finally said. "Invoice lists: Reconstructed Edison electric chair, one notebook of unknown origin, handwritten." He frowned. "That could be it."

"Have you seen it?" Sue asked.

John shook his head. "No. It never made it to the archive or research departments. George may still be reviewing it, but this is odd. It should've been cataloged months ago."

He picked up his office phone and dialed. The women held their breath.

"Hello, George," John said after a pause. "It's John. Can you come to my office for a few minutes? I have a question for you."

Whatever reply came through the receiver made John nod once. "Thanks." He hung up.

Ellen's stomach twisted as she wondered if a direct confrontation was the right approach, but before she could say anything, there was a knock at the door.

"Come in," John said.

George Flint stepped inside, his beard slightly disheveled, his badge clipped to his sweater. His eyes flicked to Ellen and her friends, and though his expression stayed cordial, Ellen saw the subtle stiffening of his shoulders.

"Ladies," George said, "good to see you again. John, you wanted to see me?"

John turned his monitor so George could see. "This notebook of unknown origin, handwritten, that came in with the electric chair—where is it? What exactly is it?"

George's face flushed, then paled. "Oh, that. I haven't finished processing it yet. It's tough to read, very dense. Probably just old research notes. I didn't think it was a priority."

John raised a brow. "I'd like to see it."

"Of course," George said quickly. "But I believe I left it in my home office. I didn't want to risk leaving it here. The cleaners aren't always careful. If you'd like, I can bring it to you first thing in the morning."

John's expression didn't waver. "I'd prefer you go get it now. I'll wait."

George blinked. "Now? Really? I mean, it's not that interesting. But if you insist—"

"I insist," John said, tone cool and steady.

George opened his mouth, then closed it again. He gave an awkward little bow. "Very well. I'll be back shortly."

The door clicked shut behind him.

Sue waited all of three seconds before saying, "We need to follow him. He's up to something."

John looked troubled. "He'll recognize my vehicle."

"I've got that covered," Tanya said, pulling out her phone. Her fingers flew across the screen. "Texting C.W. now."

Ellen exhaled, her nerves buzzing. What was George Flint up to?

The hallway outside the executive offices at the Henry Ford Museum was quiet, save for the soft hum of overhead lights and the faint creak of the old floorboards beneath their shoes. Ellen, Sue, and Tanya tiptoed down the corridor like a trio of amateur spies, their backs pressed to the wall as they eyed the closed door to George Flint's office.

"There he goes," Ellen whispered, watching as George disappeared behind his door.

They ducked behind a large potted Ficus near the water cooler. It wasn't much cover, but it was all they had.

"What's taking so long?" Tanya muttered, adjusting the strap of her crossbody bag.

"How should I know?" Sue whispered back, craning her neck to peek around the plant. "Maybe he's writing a farewell letter to his conscience."

Footsteps echoed behind them. All three women stiffened.

A woman in a sharp navy pantsuit rounded the corner, her heels clicking authoritatively against the floor. She paused when she saw them huddled together.

"Do you ladies need help?" she asked, raising a suspicious eyebrow.

Sue straightened and nodded with a bright smile. "We're the plant people."

"Plant people?" the woman echoed.

"Yes," Ellen said quickly. "We're checking the office plants for fungi. You know, mold, root rot, leaf blight—the usual."

The woman blinked.

"New initiative," Ellen added, trying not to sound like she was lying through her teeth.

"Hmm," the woman said, then nodded. "Carry on." She continued down the hall without another glance.

As soon as she was out of earshot, Tanya turned to Sue. "Plant people?"

Sue shrugged. "Hey, it worked."

"Thank goodness one of us knew something about plants," Ellen said beneath her breath.

A few seconds later, George's office door opened. The trio flattened themselves against the wall. Holding their breath, they watched him lock his office door and stride in the opposite direction without noticing their presence. He headed toward the stairwell.

After he was out of sight, Ellen exhaled. "That was too close."

They crept to the stairwell and peered down in time to see George exit the building. They slipped outside through a side door and ducked behind a manicured shrub.

Across the parking lot, George walked briskly to a white Crown Victoria.

"Come on, C.W.," Tanya murmured, glancing at her phone.

"It's a good thing John gave us Flint's address," Ellen said. "Otherwise, we'd lose him."

"There he goes," Sue pointed. George pulled out of the lot and turned onto Michigan Avenue."

A minute later, a familiar white SUV pulled up.

"We're in a hurry," Tanya said, climbing onto the front passenger's seat.

"Follow that Crown Vic!" Sue cried from the back seat.

"We playing spies now?" C.W. asked as he pulled onto the road.

"Not playing," Ellen said. "This is serious."

"Oh, wow," he muttered, gripping the wheel.

The traffic light ahead was about to turn red.

"We can't lose him, C.W.!" Tanya cried.

"I'm not driving a spaceship," he grumbled. "I can't fly through traffic."

As soon as the light turned green, C.W. pulled forward. "I refuse to drive over the speed limit, ladies. I'm sorry, but it's against my principles to break the law."

Ellen and Sue glanced at one another in the back seat.

"Well, hell," Sue murmured.

"I see him up ahead!" Tanya cried. "He's there, at the stop sign."

"At least he's using his blinker," C.W. commented. "He can't be all that bad."

They followed George another few miles down a major thoroughfare.

"We're lucky he's not driving over the limit, either," Sue groaned.

"Like I said," C.W. began, "he can't be that bad."

Ellen wasn't so sure.

Finally, George turned into a quiet residential street and pulled into the driveway of a modest brick colonial. C.W. parked across the street, one house down.

Ellen, Sue, and Tanya crouched low as they crept along a line of hedges toward the house.

"This is insane," Ellen whispered.

"It's thrilling," Sue replied. "Almost as exciting as winning the grand on Mo Mummy."

They reached a side window just in time to see George enter his study. He opened a drawer in his desk, pulled out a worn notebook from inside his jacket, and slipped it into the drawer.

"He's not *retrieving* the diary," Ellen whispered. "He's *hiding* it!"

"I wonder what he's going to tell John?" Sue said.

Suddenly, Tanya tripped over a low garden hose and fell into a bush with a loud rustle and an involuntary holler.

The women ducked.

Inside, George turned toward the window. Ellen held her breath and silently prayed as she watched him.

After a tense moment, George turned back, grabbed his car keys, and exited the study.

"He's leaving," Ellen said. "Let's move."

Once George drove off, the trio crept through a side gate and entered the backyard—only to be greeted by two yapping dachshunds.

"Oh, no," Tanya groaned.

"Nice doggies," Sue said, bending over and offering her hand. The dogs barked louder.

"They hate us," Ellen whispered.

"We need to make this quick," Tanya hissed.

They tried the back door. It was locked, but Tanya found the window next to it cracked open. It was high and narrow, like a bathroom or kitchen sink window.

"Boost me," she said as she pulled the window up.

Ellen and Sue clasped their hands to make a step. Tanya hoisted herself up, wiggled through the narrow window, and fell into the kitchen sink. A moment later, she unlocked the back door.

"Thank goodness one of us is in shape," Ellen muttered.

They hurried inside, closing the door against the yapping dogs. Then, they hastened through a messy living room to the front of the house, where they reached the office. Sue opened the drawer and pulled out the notebook.

"Got it," Sue said.

Ellen took it and flipped through it. The pages were filled with dense handwriting and diagrams. "It's definitely Edison's."

"Read it later," Tanya urged. "Let's go before he comes back!"

They rushed out the back door, past the yapping dogs, and ducked back through the gate. Then they scurried along the line of shrubs and raced across the street to C.W., who was waiting in the car.

"I hope you ladies aren't breaking any laws," he said, raising his brows.

"It's for an important cause," Ellen insisted as they climbed in.

"Where to?" he asked.

"Dearborn Inn," Sue replied. "We have some reading to do."

As they drove, Sue's phone rang.

"It's John," she said. "Putting him on speaker."

"You won't believe this," John said over the line. "George Flint just came into my office and resigned. Says he can't find the notebook and didn't want to be fired over it."

"Well, we have news, too," Sue replied. "We just stole it."

"The notebook?" John asked with astonishment.

"From his house," Ellen clarified.

"We're headed back to the inn to read it," Sue added.

"I'm on my way," John said. "I should probably file a complaint against Flint first, just in case."

"Good idea," Sue replied.

They ended the call.

C.W. glanced in the rearview mirror. "You think George Flint would do anything drastic to get that notebook back?"

The three friends looked at one another.

"I guess we're about to find out," Sue said.

<u>CHAPTER EIGHTEEN</u>

The Secret Diary

Ellen shut the door of the Patrick Henry House behind them, the soft click of the latch oddly loud in the quiet entryway. Tanya dropped her purse on the hallway table while Sue pulled off her boots with a groan.

"I feel like I've just committed a federal crime," Tanya said, holding the leather-bound notebook in both hands like it might burn her.

"You sort of have," Sue replied, flopping back against the couch. "But in our defense, he was, too."

Ellen didn't reply. She was too focused on the object in Tanya's hands—the notebook they'd snatched from George Flint's home. It looked so unassuming, just a battered old book with a cracked spine and a faint smell of mildew. But inside, Ellen knew, were answers. And maybe something worse.

"I'll order lunch," Ellen said, pulling out her phone. "No way am I reading a haunted book on an empty stomach."

"What are we hungry for?" Tanya wondered. "Sandwiches?"

"Sounds good to me," Sue replied.

Tanya headed for the sitting room's bay window and flopped into a plush chair while Ellen scrolled through the DoorDash app and ordered sandwiches and iced tea from a local deli. Once the order was placed, she set her phone aside and joined the others. Tanya laid the book on the coffee table and opened it slowly, reverently, as if expecting something to leap out of it.

The first page was filled with tightly packed writing, slanted and spidery. Tanya squinted. "I can't read a word of this. Is it even in English?"

Sue leaned over for a look. "Looks like a chicken got drunk and ran across the page."

Ellen chuckled. "After three decades of grading papers, I've gotten pretty good at decoding bad handwriting." She reached for the book. "Let me have a try."

Tanya handed it over gladly. Ellen adjusted her readers and bent low over the page. The ink had faded, and the writing, cramped and uneven, sometimes trailed off into barely visible scratches. But after a minute or two, her brain began to click into gear, untangling the slashes and curls.

"It's definitely Edison's," she said. "There are references to Menlo Park, his lab assistants, even notes on experiments. But the focus here," she turned a few pages, "is the necrophone."

"Is it a blueprint?" Tanya asked. "Like, for how it works?"

"It's more like a stream-of-consciousness diary," Ellen said. "Rambling, obsessive. He keeps going back to the same themes—sound vibration, ethereal conduction, electromagnetic barriers." She flipped through several pages, skimming quickly. "His writing really is awful. I wonder if it got worse with age."

"Everything else seems to," Sue said. "I just bought a new bra for these puppies," she cupped her breasts, "because all my others couldn't keep up."

Tanya laughed. "I know what you mean. I don't have nearly as much as you in that department, but what I do have is falling."

"I thought you said you were giving up on bras," Ellen reminded her.

"That didn't last," Tanya admitted. "They're turning into pendulums."

Ellen and Sue laughed before Ellen returned her attention to the notebook. "His writing deteriorates the further I go. These pages . . . they're odious. Fixated on bridging realms. Almost frantic." She hesitated, then added, "I honestly don't know how George Flint could have used this to control Edison's ghost. The man sounds unhinged near the end."

Sue crossed her arms. "Keep looking. There has to be more in there than schematics and ramblings."

Ellen flipped ahead, letting the pages blur beneath her fingertips, until something caught her eye.

"Hold on," she said.

"What?" Tanya asked.

"The tone shifts here. It's neater, clearer, like he's writing directly to someone." Ellen squinted. "'Dear Charles, Please rip out these pages and burn them after reading them.'"

The room went still.

"Do you think he's referring to his son Charles?" Tanya asked, voice hushed.

"I think so," Ellen said. "I remember learning that he worked closely with him."

"Either Charles never found these pages," Sue murmured, "or he didn't do what his father asked."

Ellen turned the page and began to read aloud.

Dear Charles,

I can feel my life winding down, like a phonograph needle skating toward the last groove. The world is quieter now, and I find myself with too much time to think. Too much time to remember. I have done things—terrible things—in the name of progress and pride. And now I must unburden myself, if only to you.

I waged a war against alternating current not because I feared it, but because I feared being surpassed. I allowed my name to be tied to horrors—the electric chair among them—in the hope that people would associate AC power with death. I misled the public. I tarnished the names of Westinghouse and Tesla, men who only sought to better the world in ways I could not control.

You were just a boy when I brought that poor dog into the lab. I made you and the others watch. I told myself it was science. But it was fear. I needed them to be afraid. I needed to win.

I gave false information to reporters and colleagues, made a horrible spectacle of the electrocution of Topsy the elephant, and made the film available in coin-operated kinetoscopes everywhere. I told people that Tesla's coils would destroy their homes and minds. I sent letters to government men warning them of Westinghouse's recklessness.

Guglielmo Marconi once called me the greatest benefactor of the modern world. If he had known what I had done behind closed doors, I think he would've taken those words back.

I allowed competition to consume me. The desire to be first, to be best—it blinded me. I became something I no longer recognized. Something I now fear.

Please, Charles. Burn these pages. Let my sins end with me. But do not abandon the work I described before this letter. The necrophone can answer the question in every man's heart about life after death. I hope this final invention can make up for my terrible failings.

Forgive me, if you can.

Your Loving Father,

Thomas A. Edison

For a few moments, none of them moved. The only sound was the distant hum of traffic outside the window.

Sue swallowed hard. "Well. That was . . . not what I expected."

Tanya leaned back against the sofa, one hand resting against her chest. "We just read the private confession of Thomas Edison. *The* Edison. That letter was never meant to be found by anyone other than his son, Charles."

"And it certainly wasn't meant to be used against him," Ellen said. "George Flint is blackmailing a ghost with a secret that was supposed to be destroyed."

"We have to let him know," Sue said, sitting up. "We have the journal now. Flint doesn't. Edison's ghost is free."

"And maybe he can finally help us shut the dang portal," Tanya added.

Just then, a sharp knock rattled the front door.

"That should be John," Tanya said as she went to the front window. She parted the curtain with two fingers and peered outside. She went pale. "It's not John. It's George Flint."

Ellen stood. "Are you sure?"

"I see his car. And his face." Tanya looked back at them, eyes wide with panic. "What do we do?"

"Stall him," Ellen said, already reaching for her phone. "Don't open the door. Just tell him we'll be right there."

"I'll call John," Sue said, pulling out her own phone.

Tanya tiptoed to the door and called out, "Just a minute!"

"Ladies," George's voice came from outside, muffled but unmistakably tense, "I know you have it. I just want to talk."

Ellen dialed 9-1-1 and whispered to the dispatcher, "We're at the Patrick Henry House at Dearborn Inn. A man is trying to break in. He's dangerous."

"I'll send someone now," the dispatcher assured her. "Please remain on the line."

Just then, Tanya yelped. George had managed to crack the door open slightly. Before Tanya could stop him, he shoved it wide, forcing her backward.

"Give me the journal!" he shouted, storming into the front room.

Tanya stumbled and fell to the floor. "Hey!"

"Leave her alone!" Ellen cried, combing the room for a weapon.

George's face was red, furious. "You don't know what you're doing. That book doesn't belong to you."

Sue lunged forward and threw a lamp at him. It hit his shoulder with a thud, but he barely flinched.

"Split up!" Ellen yelled.

The three women scattered. George lunged after Ellen, but she darted through the hallway and slammed the door to the kitchen behind her. She heard the sound of running footsteps—maybe Tanya upstairs, Sue to the master bath?

"What's happening?" the voice over her 9-1-1 call asked. "Are you okay?"

Before Ellen could answer, George kicked the kitchen door with a loud crash. "You don't understand! Edison's work on the portal is nearly complete!"

Ellen scrambled through the kitchen and ducked into the pantry. She pulled the door shut and held her breath.

She heard him enter the kitchen, footsteps clapping on tile.

"Where are you?" he called out.

Ellen's phone buzzed in her pocket. She fumbled to silence it. A text from Sue: *I'm in the laundry room. You okay?*

Ellen started typing a reply when the pantry door jerked open.

George loomed in the doorway, eyes wild. "Give it to me!"

"I don't have it!" she insisted.

His hands reached for her—but just then, a loud *thwack* echoed through the house, followed by a yell.

"Stop, you maniac!" Sue shouted from behind him, her gun pointed at him.

Then: *sirens.*

George's expression changed. He backed away, chest heaving. "You called the cops."

"Darn right we did," Tanya said, appearing beside Sue with a fireplace poker.

George spun around, startled, and bolted toward the front of the house. But it was too late. Blue and red lights danced through the windows. A voice called out from the porch, "This is the Dearborn Police! Come out with your hands up!"

George hesitated only a moment before raising his hands and walking out.

Ellen collapsed against the pantry wall, her legs trembling.

Tanya rushed over and helped her up. "Are you okay?"

"I think so," Ellen said. "Where's the journal?"

Sue appeared in the doorway, the leather-bound notebook clutched against her chest like a life raft. "Safe."

Outside, they heard officers shouting and handcuffing George. A minute later, John Coleman burst through the front door, breathless and wild-eyed.

He looked around the room, taking in the disarray. "Are you all okay?"

"We will be," Ellen said. She reached for the journal, took it from Sue, and held it out to him. "But you need to read this."

John took it, though he didn't open it yet. "Did George hurt any of you?"

"He shoved Tanya and chased us around like a lunatic," Sue said. "But we're okay. It's a good thing I had my gun."

John exhaled. "He won't be bothering anyone again. The police said he'll be held for breaking and entering and assault. And if you're willing to testify, he won't be back at Greenfield Village either."

"Oh, we're willing," Tanya said.

"More than willing," Sue added.

Ellen looked at the journal, now resting in John's hands. "The things he used to blackmail Edison . . . they were never meant to be seen. Edison's last wishes were to burn those pages."

John nodded solemnly. "Then it's a good thing they're in the right hands now."

Ellen looked at her friends. "Now that Flint is out of the picture, it's time to go back to the Farris Windmill."

"And talk to Edison," Sue said.

"Maybe now," Tanya added, "he'll be willing to help us close the portal."

At that moment, a man carrying a large plastic sack walked up the sidewalk. "Did someone here order DoorDash?"

"Our lunch!" Ellen cried with a laugh. "I totally forgot!"

"I don't think I can eat," Tanya muttered as she sat down on the sofa.

"Well, I can," Sue said, reaching for the sack. "Stress eating is my superpower."

CHAPTER NINETEEN

Motown and Momentum

Later that afternoon, Ellen removed her reading glasses in the back seat next to Sue as C.W. pulled up in front of the unassuming white-and-blue house that once changed the world.

"Is that it?" Tanya asked, peering through the front passenger's window. "It looks like someone's grandma still lives there."

"That's because someone's grandma probably *did* live there," C.W. replied. "Between recording hits."

The sign above the porch read *Hitsville U.S.A.*, the original home of Motown Records.

"We are standing at the birthplace of *soul*, ladies," C.W. added as Ellen and her friends climbed out of the car.

"That's right," Ellen chastised. "Let's show some reverence."

"Reverence?" Sue grinned. "I came to sing."

"I'm not surprised," Tanya muttered, tugging her cardigan tighter against the chill in the air.

"I'll be right here when you're ready," C.W. said with a wave as the three friends walked off.

The front door opened, and a young man with a slick ponytail and infectious smile greeted them. "Welcome to Hitsville! You're just in time for the last tour of the day."

Inside, the air felt heavy with nostalgia. Posters of Smokey Robinson, The Supremes, Marvin Gaye, and Stevie Wonder lined the hallway. Original vinyl records gleamed from glass cases. The guide led them past Berry Gordy's apartment-turned-office, explaining how he'd mortgaged his house to start Motown with an $800 loan.

"Now *that's* what I call hustle," Sue whispered to Ellen.

They entered a narrow studio lined with acoustic tiles. A baby grand piano stood in one corner, flanked by a drum set and a mic on a stand.

"This," the guide said with reverence, "is Studio A, the Hit Factory. Almost every Motown hit from 1959 to 1972 was recorded right here."

Ellen's chest tightened with something like awe. She could *feel* the layers of sound still vibrating in the floorboards—baselines, tambourines, harmonies. Echoes of brilliance.

"Who wants to step up to the mic and test it out?" the guide asked, half-teasing.

Without missing a beat, Sue raised her hand. "Oh, *I* do."

Tanya groaned. "Oh no."

"Let her," Ellen said, nudging Tanya with a grin. "She's been itching to unleash her inner Supreme all week."

Sue strutted up to the mic like she'd done it a hundred times before. "This one goes out to all the ghosts still grooving in the walls," she said.

Then she belted: "Stop! In the name of love . . ."

Her voice rang out—rich, bold, and slightly flat.

A few tourists clapped. Ellen jumped in with, "Before you break my heart!"

Tanya crossed her arms. "I swear, if you make me sing back-up—"

Sue gave her the eye. "Oh, come on. Don't act like you don't know the choreography."

With an exaggerated sigh, Tanya stepped forward, reluctantly mimicking the classic arm movement—*Stop!*—in perfect time.

By the time they sang the chorus, even the guide was swaying.

Ellen laughed until her stomach hurt. Here they were, three women in their sixties, mid-paranormal investigation, singing their hearts out in one of the most sacred studios in music history.

Somehow, it made perfect sense.

After the applause and a few photo ops, they moved back toward the museum's final exhibits. As the crowd dispersed, Ellen lingered near a timeline showing the evolution of Motown's influence through the Civil Rights era. Something about it—the momentum of that era, the courage, the creativity—struck a chord deep inside her.

"Hey," Sue said, stepping beside her. "You okay?"

"I'm just thinking," Ellen replied. "All this started from one man's dream and a whole lot of faith."

Sue lifted a brow. "Kind of like us."

Tanya joined them, holding her phone. "All right, rock stars. We've got a dinner reservation in thirty minutes. Grand Trunk Pub. Let's go before Sue tries to start a flash mob."

Sue fluffed her bangs. "You're just jealous of my pipes."

They exited into the cool twilight air and started down the steps, their laughter carrying into the breeze. But as they climbed back into the Uber with C.W., Ellen sobered.

Once they were buckled in and headed toward downtown, she leaned forward slightly. "Okay. Let's talk about what's next."

"You mean the part where we somehow convince a dead Thomas Edison to close a ghost portal he opened last fall?" Tanya asked.

"Yes. That part." Ellen lowered her voice, "We know George Flint no longer has control over him. That's the good news."

"But Edison's already halfway gone," Sue said. "He admitted that he's evil, *he's* the darkness."

"Which is why we need a new strategy," Ellen replied. "We have to reach what's left of his humanity."

"Appeal to his better conscience," Tanya added. "Assuming he has one."

Ellen nodded. "That letter to Charles—his confession—that showed regret. Guilt. That's what we have to tap into."

Sue crossed her arms. "We can't exactly convince him with a puppy and a TED Talk."

Ellen sighed. "No, but we *can* let him know we're not his enemies. We have his journal. We know his secret. And we want to help him make it right."

C.W. shook his head. "I don't know how you ladies do it. This sounds scary as hell to me."

"It's for a good cause," Sue piped up.

Ellen grinned. "We're not sure, but we may just be saving the world."

C.W. chuckled. "Oh, is that all?"

Tanya frowned. "You really think we can reason with a ghost who ripped a hole between realms, even though it threatens life as we know it?"

"I think we have to try," Ellen said. "Before he finishes what he started. Who knows what that looks like, what that even means. He said, 'Destroys life.'"

"Yeah," Sue said with a sigh. "I don't want to find out what that means."

The car turned onto Woodward Avenue.

Sue gave Ellen a mischievous look. "You know what we need?"

"A miracle?" Tanya guessed from the front passenger's seat.

"Wine," Sue declared. "And fries. And something with gravy. We can save the world after dessert."

Ellen chuckled. "Fair enough."

"But first," Sue added, raising an eyebrow, "can we talk about how that museum guide was definitely flirting with me?"

"He was twenty-five," Tanya said flatly.

"Exactly," Sue beamed. "I've still got it."

Ellen rolled her eyes. "You 'had it' because you sang in his sacred studio like it was karaoke night."

"You sang karaoke?" C.W. asked, his brows lifted.

"We all did," Sue replied.

"I wish I could have seen it," he said with a grin.

Sue lifted her brows at Ellen, as if to say, "I told you C.W. is into me."

Tanya snorted. "Let's hope Grand Trunk has good acoustics. Sue's going to serenade the waiter."

Their laughter filled the car as C.W. pulled up outside the converted train-station-turned-restaurant.

"Are you joining us?" Tanya asked as she opened her car door.

"Not this time, ladies. Just text when you're ready."

Ellen stepped into the Grand Trunk Pub and immediately looked up.

"Whoa," she whispered.

A soaring vaulted ceiling arched overhead, gilded with honeyed light and ringed with curved iron trusses. The old Michigan Central Railway ticket office had been transformed into a gastropub, but the bones of the station still spoke of steam trains and paper tickets and soldiers leaving for war. The amber-stained glass glowed like twilight in a cathedral.

"Now *this* is my kind of train station," Sue said, shaking off her coat. "No delays, no lost luggage, and full bar service."

Tanya adjusted her ponytail and gave an appreciative nod. "This is fancier than I expected."

"Detroit knows how to do heritage with a side of class," Ellen said.

A hostess seated them at a high-backed booth near the front window, beneath an enormous iron chandelier that looked like it had once hung over a steam engine. The table was etched with initials and tiny hearts carved into the wood over the years. Ellen ran her fingers over one of them absently: *J.T. + L.M.*

"Okay," Sue said, cracking open the menu. "Let's take this one step at a time. First, we order cocktails. Second, we order all the carbs. Third, we save the living and the dead."

Tanya looked up. "That's the actual order?"

"Absolutely. I can't fight the undead on an empty stomach."

Ellen grinned, but her thoughts had already been tugged toward the journal. They'd barely scratched the surface. Edison's guilt, his ambition, his desperation to talk to the dead—they had it all in writing now. But understanding it didn't make it easier.

Not when a portal was still open.

Not when souls—possibly of both the dead and the living—hung in the balance.

Their waiter arrived, tall and dimpled, with a flannel shirt and a tattoo of a raven on his forearm. "Welcome to Grand Trunk, ladies. Can I tempt you with some Detroit Old Fashioneds or a barrel-aged Manhattan to start?"

Sue leaned across the table like a cat about to pounce. "You had me at 'barrel-aged.' Surprise me."

"I'll take an Old Fashioned," Ellen said, offering a polite smile.

"Hot toddy," Tanya muttered. "Still chilled from that museum."

"Got it," the waiter said. "And how hungry are we talking tonight?"

"Apocalyptic," Sue answered.

"End-of-days level," Ellen added.

The waiter gave a mock salute. "Then you're in the right place."

He left, and the trio fell into a comfortable hush. Jazz music played faintly through the speakers, plinking piano notes trailing like ghosts through the air.

Tanya finally broke the silence. "So. What's the plan?"

Ellen exhaled. "First, we need to reach Edison."

Sue sipped her water. "Didn't we already do that? At the Eloise? He nearly turned me into a chalk outline."

"That wasn't *him*," Ellen said. "Not really. That was the corrupted version of him—tainted by grief, obsession, and being manipulated by Flint. But I believe he's still in there. We have to reach his humanity."

"You think he still wants to help humanity?" Tanya asked.

"I think part of him does," Ellen replied. "But I also think he's afraid. Regret can fester into shame. And he's had a hundred years to stew in it."

Sue leaned forward. "Then we have to show him he can make things right."

"Exactly," Ellen said. "But we need the *how*."

Their drinks arrived, and so did two plates of truffle fries, a skillet of mac and cheese with duck confit, and something called Motor City Meatballs served with sourdough toast.

"Now *this* is ghost-hunting fuel," Sue said, popping a fry into her mouth. "All right, let's brainstorm. How do you coax an emotionally repressed genius from the other side into helping you fix a tear in the veil between worlds?"

"Can't believe that's a sentence I understood," Tanya murmured with a roll of her eyes.

"We remind him of the man he used to be," Ellen said slowly. "The inventor. The father. The friend."

"We could reread the letter Edison wrote to Charles," Tanya suggested. "Out loud, when we know his ghost is with us."

"Yes," Ellen said, "but maybe it's not just the words—it's the *emotion* behind them. Maybe we need to recreate something that taps into his memories. A trigger."

Sue snapped her fingers. "A place. A time. A moment from his life."

"The phonograph," Ellen said quietly. "That's where it all started. We can remind Edison about the important contributions he's made—"

"And we might reach what's left of his soul," Tanya finished.

"I wonder," Ellen began with a thoughtful tilt to her head, "if we can reach the spirit of Henry Ford. They were good friends. Maybe Ford could coax Edison into doing the right thing."

"That's not a bad idea," Sue said with a nod.

"Why, thank you, Sue." Ellen grinned. "That means a lot coming from you."

"Let's just hope it works," Tanya put in. "I'm afraid to see what happens if we don't close that portal."

The table fell silent again. Outside, the city sparkled in the reflection of the pub's tall windows. Streetcars passed, headlights glowing like will-o'-the-wisps.

Sue nudged Ellen with her elbow. "What's going on in that little brain of yours?"

Ellen smiled faintly. "I'm thinking about how long we've been doing this. Ghosts. Histories. Injustices. We've faced some terrifying things."

"And we always make it out," Tanya said. "Barely."

Sue raised her glass. "To barely."

They clinked their drinks together, a muted chime that echoed beneath the arches of the old train station.

"And to our husbands," Sue added.

Ellen nearly choked on her drink. "What?"

"Come on," Sue said. "I'm trying to be nice, remember?"

"I thought you were always nice," Tanya teased.

"You know me better than that."

"To our husbands," Ellen said, clinking her glass against the glasses of her friends.

Ellen glanced at her ring finger. "Brian would've loved this place. He was obsessed with trains as a kid, and this is exactly the type of atmosphere he and his brother create at their breweries."

"Dave would've hated it," Tanya said. "Too loud. Too many hipsters. Too many pickled things on the menu."

Sue laughed. "I'm not sure Tom would have even agreed to come in the first place."

They all laughed, but it faded into something gentler.

"Getting old is weird," Sue said suddenly.

"Weirder than ghosts?" Ellen asked.

Sue nodded. "Sometimes, yeah."

Ellen took another sip of her drink. "I don't mind the wrinkles. Or the aches. It's the . . . quiet. I miss the kids. I miss Paul. Brian and I have a great time, but sometimes I miss the old days."

Tanya surprised them by reaching across the table and taking each of their hands. "Then let's keep making noise, while we can."

They held that silence for a beat, then Sue smirked.

"Well, I'll be," Sue said. "That was almost profound."

Tanya shrugged. "Don't act surprised. I can be profound."

Ellen and Sue giggled.

A server passed behind them carrying a chocolate bread pudding that smelled like heaven.

Sue tilted her head. "Now that would draw any ghost from the other realm."

Ellen blinked. "What?"

"I mean, don't you think they miss things like chocolate sauce and crispy edges?"

Tanya groaned. "If you start a ghost food truck, I'm quitting the team."

Sue grinned. "What would I call it? *Spirit Bites*?"

"*Boo-ger King*," Ellen offered.

Sue whooped with laughter. Tanya covered her face and groaned.

Ellen shook her head, laughing until tears formed at the corners of her eyes. The moment felt alive—real, human, and whole. Even with death hanging in the air. Even with a haunted windmill waiting.

When their own chocolate bread pudding came, they shared it in quiet contentment. Outside, the city moved on—oblivious to the spirits shifting beneath its surface.

They would face Edison again.

They would find a way to close the portal.

But for tonight, under a cathedral of train arches and Motown echoes, they were just three women sharing pudding and making plans.

CHAPTER TWENTY

Round Two and a Detour

The wind was biting on Tuesday morning as Ellen, Sue, and Tanya stepped out of John's Ford Explorer and walked through the gate of Greenfield Village.

"Thanks for giving us the journal back," Ellen told John as she waved goodbye. "We promise to return it when we're done with it."

They wore their gear like pack mules as they trudged along the sidewalk, past the childhood home of Henry Ford toward the entrance of Menlo Lab.

"Round two," Sue murmured, clutching the strap of her padded bag as she glanced toward the door.

"Let's hope this works," Tanya said with a sigh.

Inside, the lab was chilly and dim. The antique bulbs overhead illuminated shelves stacked with glass tubes, wires, and brass instruments. The phonograph sat proudly at the center of an exhibit by the stairs to the second floor. The machine had drawn Edison's attention before, if only faintly. Maybe it would again.

Ellen set down her bag and carefully opened the journal they had stolen from George Flint. It still gave her the chills, even now, knowing what Edison had written—not just about his invention, but his regrets. The weight of those words made this place feel holier somehow.

He had loved this workbench, this desk. He'd loved them so much that he had chosen to remain at his lab after death rather than crossing on to the other side.

Sue turned on the spirit box and placed it near the phonograph. Static hissed, filling the room with restless noise. Tanya scanned with the EMF detector, which flickered weakly before dying down again.

Ellen called out to the ghost of Thomas Edison. "We're here to help, not harm. We've recovered your secret diary from your blackmailer, George Flint. You can close the portal now."

They waited. Nothing.

"Calling Thomas Edison," Sue finally said. "Are you here? Can you give us a sign?"

More silence.

"Maybe he's at the Eloise," Ellen wondered.

"Or maybe he's mad at us," Tanya muttered. "For stealing the journal."

"Or maybe he's too far gone," Sue added quietly.

Ellen leaned over the phonograph, brushing her hand over the wood. "Thomas Alva Edison," she said softly, "we read your journal. We know you regret what happened with the chair, with Westinghouse and Tesla, and with Topsy the elephant. We want to help you. But we need your help, too."

The spirit box hissed, then stuttered. A garbled syllable, like the start of a name, broke through, then vanished.

"Was that him?" Tanya asked, eyes wide.

"Could be," Sue said. But even she sounded doubtful.

They tried the Estes method and the Ouija board but got no response from either.

Ellen paced near the desk while Sue sat on a stool, head bowed in thought. Tanya peered out the window at the quiet village paths.

Finally, Ellen exhaled. "I think we need to try again later. Spirits are always more active after sunset."

"So, we come back after dark," Tanya said. "What do we do until then?"

Sue stood and stretched. "Nap? Eat? Think about how we talk a ghost into saving the world?"

"Oh!" Tanya snapped her fingers. "We could visit the Basilica of Sainte Anne and the old Michigan Central Station. C.W. said that those are places we must see!"

"Good idea, Tanya," Ellen praised, tucking the journal into her bag.

"I guess that means no nap," Sue murmured.

"We can drop you off first, if you want," Tanya offered.

"And miss out? No, thanks."

Ellen looked around the lab one last time before flipping off the spirit box. "Hang on, Mr. Edison. We'll be back tonight."

The wind had picked up again by the time they exited Menlo Lab, their hopes tangled in disappointment. Ellen buttoned her coat all the way up and glanced toward the cloudy sky. Even March in Michigan didn't pull its punches.

"I still think he was there," Sue murmured as she buckled into the backseat of C.W.'s white SUV. "He just wasn't ready."

"Or maybe we're not ready," Tanya said from the front passenger's seat.

Ellen settled in the back beside Sue. "C.W., is your offer to show us the church and railroad museum still open?"

C.W. grinned at them in the rearview mirror. "Absolutely. Where to first: church or trains?"

"Church," Sue said. "Always good to hedge our bets."

The Basilica of Sainte Anne de Detroit rose like a solemn sentinel from the edge of the riverfront, its towering twin spires reaching for the sky with French Gothic flair. As they approached, Ellen felt a gentle hush descend over her mind, quieting the rush of plans and fears that had gripped her since morning. She felt a sense of awe as she followed the others up the path to the church.

"This place is older than the United States," C.W. said as he held open the church door. "Founded in 1701. Same year Detroit was born."

Inside, the basilica was breathtaking. Sunlight streamed through the intricate stained-glass windows, painting the marble floors in rose, sapphire, and gold. Wooden pews lined the nave, and the cathedral ceiling was comprised of arches painted in sky blue and gold.

"Wow," Tanya whispered.

They wandered down the center aisle, letting their footsteps echo beneath the arches. Ellen paused beside a shrine to Sainte Anne, candles flickering in the shadow of the stone.

"She's the patron saint of grandmothers," C.W. said softly, noticing Ellen's gaze.

"Well, *I'm* a grandmother," Ellen said. "I even have the hips for it."

Tanya sighed. "I wish I had grandkids *and* hips."

"You're perfect the way you are," Ellen reassured her.

"Except for that attitude," Sue teased. "That could be improved upon."

Ellen shook her head. "And you *will* be a grandmother, Tanya, one of these days. You know Camie was meant to be a mom."

They continued their exploration. Tanya lingered near a side chapel, her hands clasped in front of her. The echo of an organ rehearsal began, soft chords blooming into the air. Ellen sat in one of the pews and closed her eyes for a moment.

She remembered the tall, shadowy figure they saw—not once, but twice—at the Eloise. The Hat Man. She hoped they could give Edison a reason to care again. To choose humanity again.

The organ music shifted into something recognizable—*Amazing Grace*—and Ellen opened her eyes to find Sue humming along.

"Feel better?" C.W. asked once they'd exited into the chill again.

"Spiritually recalibrated," Sue said. "But I could use something with less incense."

"Next stop," C.W. began, "railroads."

The drive through Detroit was quiet for a time, each of them staring out their windows. Without the calming effect of the church, Ellen mulled over the unsatisfying encounter with Edison's spirit. She had hoped for something more—some spark of recognition, some clue to guide them. Instead, all they got was static, a garbled word, and a sense that Edison's ghost had retreated into bitterness.

She sighed and watched as the imposing silhouette of the station came into view, its Beaux-Arts architecture rising like a cathedral against the overcast sky.

"Oh my," Ellen murmured. "It looks like something out of an old noir film."

Sue leaned forward in her seat. "This place is huge. Didn't I read somewhere it was the tallest train station in the world when it opened?"

"Sure was," C.W. said as he pulled into a small parking lot. "1913. Henry Ford used it. Presidents passed through it. Then it was abandoned for decades until Ford Motor Company bought it back and restored it."

"Full circle," Tanya muttered as she stepped out. "Henry Ford again."

Inside, the station was a breathtaking blend of industrial grandeur and meticulous restoration. Sunlight filtered through the massive arched windows, glinting off the tiny tiles on the ceiling, arranged in a herringbone pattern. The walls gleamed with polished stone and brass fixtures, reflected in the shiny, cream, marble floors. A massive crystal chandelier hung in what was once the ticket lobby, illuminating a clock that C.W. said was a reproduction of the original.

"I feel like I should be wearing gloves and a hat," Ellen whispered as they crossed the wide expanse. "This place demands elegance."

"You should see it at night," C.W. said. "It's beautiful. They light the windows up in blues and golds. Feels like stepping into history."

They wandered beneath the high vaulted ceilings and past the restored ticket counters and remnants of waiting rooms now converted into gallery spaces. Tanya paused beside an old wooden bench and ran her hand along its smooth armrest.

"You know," Sue said, "if I were a spirit with unfinished business, I might linger here. Think of all the hellos and goodbyes spoken on this floor."

Ellen nodded slowly, drawn to a massive brass schedule board above the main terminal. Though it was no longer functional, someone had carefully arranged the letters to spell out a message:

WELCOME BACK TO THE FUTURE OF DETROIT.

C.W. joined her side. "This place might be more than just a pretty detour. Ford put a lot of care into this building. Maybe it's another thread you could use tonight—to reach him."

Ellen's lifted her brows. "That's not a bad idea. Henry Ford cared deeply about legacy. Maybe this station—its resurrection—might stir something."

Sue clapped her hands. "Then let's grab photos. Energy loves familiarity, right? Maybe something here will resonate."

They spent another half hour exploring, taking pictures of original fixtures, walking along the tracks behind the station where freight trains once thundered through. The south concourse had a glass ceiling, allowing even more light to spill in and cascade off the cream tiles and polished stone. Tanya found an old conductor's cap in a display case and made Sue pose in front of it like a train engineer.

Another section, also bright, was covered in plaster made to look like tile. C.W. explained that it was once a restaurant for fine dining.

As they exited, Ellen glanced back once more at the lobby, wondering what it must have been like in its heyday—families embracing, soldiers boarding trains, businessmen in coats and fedoras tipping their hats to women in gloves.

Back in the car, C.W. pulled away from the curb. "So, what's next?"

"How about dinner?" Ellen said. "C.W., care to join us?"

"It would be my pleasure."

"Oh, the trigger objects!" Tanya reminded them. "C.W., would you mind running us by the Henry Ford Museum first? We need to pick up a few things from John Coleman."

"That would be my pleasure, too."

Grey Ghost Detroit buzzed with the low hum of conversation and clinking glassware, the kind of atmospheric soundtrack Ellen found oddly comforting. Industrial light fixtures hung from the ceiling like halos above reclaimed wood tables and black leather booths. The exposed brick walls and open kitchen gave the space a gritty elegance—like the city itself, polished through resilience.

Ellen slid into a booth across from C.W., whom she and her friends had insisted on treating to dinner as a thank-you for being their personal chauffeur. Sue slid beside C.W., already eyeing the cocktail menu, while Tanya perched beside Ellen, removing her coat with a dramatic sigh.

"Well," Sue said, smoothing her hair, "if the Basilica didn't save our souls, this menu might."

Ellen smiled, though her thoughts drifted back to the soaring stained glass of Sainte Anne's and the ghost of hope she felt there—an almost imperceptible flicker of something holy. But it was fleeting, like most things lately.

A server arrived, setting down glasses of water and welcoming them with a grin. "Any questions about the menu?"

"Do you have anything that can make us forget unpleasant things?" Tanya asked, deadpan.

The server chuckled. "Our cocktails are strong, and our steak is divine."

"We'll start there," C.W. said with a wink, then turned to Ellen. "You okay? You've been quiet since the station."

Ellen shrugged, studying the menu but not really seeing it. "Just thinking."

"We all are," Sue added gently. "Tonight's a big deal."

That was putting it mildly. They'd seen ghosts before—spoken to them, helped them, even argued with them—but this was different. Reaching Edison's humanity felt like a turning point. Not just for the case, but maybe for him. Maybe for all of them.

"I'll have the dry-aged ribeye," Sue said suddenly, setting her menu down with finality. "If I'm going to be electrocuted for the sake of science, I want red meat first."

C.W. raised his eyebrows. "She's joking, right?"

"Not really," Tanya said.

"I'll do the scallops," Ellen said finally. "With the charred leeks."

The others placed their orders—C.W. chose the fried bologna sliders and the double cheeseburger, and Tanya went for the roasted chicken with truffle grits.

When their drinks arrived—Old Fashioneds for Ellen and C.W., a margarita for Sue, and a glass of red for Tanya—they toasted with solemn smiles.

"To the ghosts," Tanya said.

"To the truth," added Sue.

"To surviving whatever comes next," Ellen murmured.

They clinked glasses.

Dinner arrived like a sensory balm. The plates were small masterpieces—the steak perfectly seared, Ellen's scallops buttery and tender, the roasted vegetables seasoned to perfection. For a few quiet minutes, they simply ate. Ellen savored every bite, letting the textures and flavors ground her.

C.W. broke the silence first. "I still can't believe that Edison is your ghost."

"Most people think of him as the light-bulb guy," Tanya said as she cut into her roasted chicken.

Ellen pushed her plate slightly away, her appetite waning. "I hope we can reach him. I hate to think about what happens if we can't."

"I think," C.W. said, wiping his mouth with a napkin, "that if anyone can reach him, it's you three. You've got his journal, and you've made a lot of progress, uncovering the existence of the portal and the role that wicked curator played in it. You ladies have got this."

Ellen chuckled softly, grateful for the levity. But deep down, she wasn't so sure. Edison had buried his guilt for over a century. What if it had become part of him?

Dessert came uninvited—a surprise gift from the kitchen. A generous slab of banana bread pudding with bourbon caramel and brown sugar whipped cream.

"See?" Sue said, scooping a bite. "Even in a haunted city, there are sweet things."

They passed the dish around like it was communion.

As they left the restaurant, night fell fully over Detroit. The air was thick with the scent of exhaust and possibility. Ellen looked toward the skyline, where the silhouette of the train station loomed in the distance like a relic from a dream.

"You were right," Ellen said to C.W. as she climbed in the back seat of his white SUV.

"About what?" he asked, waiting to close her door.

"The station really is beautiful at night."

C.W. smiled and climbed behind the wheel before he pulled away from the restaurant parking lot.

From the front passenger's seat, Tanya said, "So, what if Edison refuses to help even after we plead our hearts out?"

"We'll find another way," Sue said from the back seat beside Ellen. "But I have to believe the man who invented the phonograph, who cared about communication and memory and legacy, can be reached."

Ellen nodded. "If he's truly gone, we'll know. But if even a spark of him remains . . ."

"Then you'll light the fire," C.W. finished.

<u>CHAPTER TWENTY-ONE</u>

Searching for Edison's Humanity

The night had chilled by the time Ellen, Sue, and Tanya returned to Greenfield Village. Shadows draped the historic buildings like old velvet curtains, thick and solemn. The lanterns lining the walkways glowed with a soft amber light, but Menlo Lab stood darker than the rest—eerily quiet, still, and waiting.

"Well," Sue said as she stepped out of C.W.'s car, "in every horror movie, this is when you get killed."

Tanya adjusted her scarf. "And yet here we are. Again."

Ellen took the lead, her boots clapping lightly against the pavement. She and her friends carried the bags containing their investigative equipment over their shoulders as they entered the gate and trudged toward the lab. She didn't like the feel of the night. It was too quiet.

The three women approached the lab's entrance. The door creaked open, and the scent of oil, metal, and time greeted them like a breath from another century.

Inside, the lab looked much as it had that morning. Workbenches cluttered with tools. Shelves brimming with dusty glass tubes and coils. But the atmosphere felt denser now—like the air itself was charged.

Sue turned on the overhead light—strings of incandescent bulbs reminiscent of the first designed by Edison. Then, the ladies began setting up their equipment: positioning full-spectrum cameras, the spirit box, an EMF detector, and other devices around the lab. Although it was bulky, Ellen had asked C.W. to stop at the Patrick Henry House on the way, so she could pick up her electromagnetic generator. It would feed the spirits with electric energy, hopefully making it easier for them to communicate.

Tanya turned on the spirit box. Static filled the air, jittery and chaotic.

Ellen approached the phonograph. "I suppose we need to wind this up, like Leroy did the other day."

Tanya took something from a back shelf. "First we need to add this cylinder to the machine, remember?"

After Tanya was done, Ellen lowered the needle onto the wax cylinder.

As Sue cranked the wheel, she said, "Spirits of the other realm, we come in peace. I'm Sue, and these are my friends, Tanya and Ellen. We're hoping to speak with the ghost of Thomas Edison. Sometimes you go by Al. Thomas Alva Edison, are you here?"

A hiss. A few cracks. Then a voice, subtle but clear came over the phonograph: "Mary had a little lamb, its fleece was white as snow."

The sound was chilling, but it was the confirmation they were looking for.

"Thank goodness," Tanya whispered.

"Thomas Alva Edison," Ellen said, stepping forward. "We have your diary. You're free from George Flint. We read what you wrote to your son. We know you regret what you did, and we promise not to share it with the world."

Static flared over the spirit box.

Sue stopped cranking the phonograph and reached for the notebook. She held it up so any watching presence could see it. "You can stop now with the portal. No one is making you open it anymore."

The spirit box crackled before saying, "No . . . quitter."

Ellen's spine tingled. "You're not a quitter," she said gently. "But maybe now's the time to let go. Not of your legacy—of your guilt."

A long silence. Then: "Chair."

The word sliced through the static like a razor.

Tanya drew in a sharp breath. "He means the electric chair."

Ellen nodded slowly. "You thought you were doing the right thing. But fear and pride led you astray. It happens to all of us. We make choices we regret. The only way forward is to forgive ourselves."

Another pause, then: "Can't."

"Can't," Tanya repeated. "He can't forgive himself."

One of the glass jars crashed to the floor, causing all three ladies to flinch.

"Not again," Ellen groaned.

"Let's try to call on Henry Ford," Sue suggested. "If Ford's spirit can forgive him, maybe Edison can forgive himself."

Ellen and Tanya nodded in agreement as they pulled out their phones and opened photos they'd taken at the Michigan Central Station, hoping to trigger Henry Ford.

Sue stepped forward and spoke clearly into the air, "Henry Ford, if you're listening, your friend Thomas Edison needs you. We need your help to reach him."

"We need the trigger objects," Ellen said as she rummaged through her bag.

"Oh, yeah!" Tanya helped Ellen to set out the items they had picked up from John before dining at Grey Ghost Detroit.

Ellen found the copy of Ford's original $5 workday announcement to remind Ford of the compassion he showed his workers when he doubled their pay and reduced their hours. She put it on the antique desk beside them, where Sue had put three pillar candles.

Tanya laid the Model T radiator cap beside it, along with a copy of Ford's autobiography, *My Life and Work*.

Sue called out, "Henry Ford, do you remember your $5 workday announcement? You changed a lot of lives that day. We have a copy of the original."

They waited a few minutes but found only silence.

Tanya lifted the radiator cap. "And this is from one of your earliest Model Ts. Like your friend Thomas Edison, you changed the world for the better, and we need your help in helping your friend."

Again, they waited, again nothing.

"Maybe if we read a few lines from his autobiography, we can get his attention," Ellen suggested.

"Good idea," Sue whispered.

Ellen picked up the book and skimmed through its pages. Then, she read, "'The man who will use his skill and constructive imagination to see how much he can give for a dollar, instead of how little he can give for a dollar, is bound to succeed.' That was your philosophy, Henry. You cared about people. You built more than cars. You built lives."

When nothing happened, Tanya whispered, "Try again."

Ellen flipped through the pages and settled on this: "'I have tried to live in such a way that, when I die, someone can say, "he cared."' And that's exactly what we're saying now, Henry Ford. You cared. That's why we're asking for your help with your friend, Edison."

The spirit box remained quiet, except for static and pulsing. Ellen flipped through the pages, muttering, "I'll try one more. Here we go: 'When I told him I had built a gasoline car, Edison banged his fist on the table and said, "Young man, that's the thing. You have it. Keep at it!"' Henry Ford, your friend encouraged you then, but he needs your encouragement now."

Suddenly, the spirit box spit out something unintelligible, followed by, "That you . . . Henry?"

Ellen and her friends exchanged excited glances.

"Is Henry Ford with us?" Sue asked.

The lights overhead flickered as the word "Yes" came over the spirit box.

"Wonderful!" Ellen cried.

Before she could ask another question, however, the static surged, then dimmed again. Then, "Tom?"

It was a different voice. Warmer.

Ellen looked up, heart racing. "Henry Ford? Is that you?"

One of the candle flames snuffed out, its smoke swirling upward the incandescent light bulbs overhead. Ellen noticed them flicker again.

"Henry Ford?" Sue repeated. "Are you here?"

"Yes," the spirit box said. Then, "Tom?"

The phonograph began to crank on its own, and the words, "Hello, hello, hello," played over it.

A chill crept down Ellen's spine as she turned to her friends. She mouthed, "It's working!"

Over the spirit box came a full sentence: "You built a bridge, Tom."

The spirit box hissed.

Ellen asked, "What bridge? Do you mean the portal?"

"Wrong kind," the spirit box replied in the voice of what they believed to be the ghost of Henry Ford.

Over the phonograph, still cranking on its own, came the words, "It was wrong. So many mistakes."

Ellen gasped. These great men from history were having a conversation with one another in the afterlife, and she and her friends were privy to it.

The spirit box crackled, "Make it right, Tom."

Sue looked up and cried, "You can close that bridge, Thomas Alva Edison, and we can help. You can fix what George Flint forced you to open."

Tanya picked up Edison's secret journal. "Remember what you wrote to your son Charles? You wrote, 'Guglielmo Marconi once called me the greatest benefactor of the modern world. If he had known what I had done behind closed doors, I think he would've taken those words back. I allowed competition to consume me. The desire to be first, to be best—it blinded me. I became something I no longer recognized. Something I now fear.' Well, Thomas Alva Edison, now's your chance to make things right. Save humanity and close that portal, before it's too late."

A pause. Then, over the phonograph: "Okay."

Tears welled in Ellen's eyes. Tanya let out a quiet sob.

Sue grinned and wiped her cheeks. "Atta boy, Edison."

The phonograph spit out another phrase: "You need to build a device to close it."

Ellen glanced at her friends. "What? Us? *We* need to build it?"

"I'll show you how," the phonograph played.

The EMF reader glowed more brightly. The spirit box crackled again: "Build . . . with care. Goodbye, Tom, old friend."

Over the phonograph, "So long, Henry."

Ellen looked at her friends, heart thudding.

"He wants us to build something?" Tanya asked with wide eyes.

"Oh, Lordy," Sue bemoaned.

CHAPTER TWENTY-TWO

A New Device

The old colonial timbers creaked like whispering ghosts as Ellen lay in bed, the blankets bunched at her ankles and her sketchbook resting on her knees. Moonlight spilled through the rippled glass panes of the window, catching the fine motes of dust drifting through the air like old memories. The Patrick Henry House had settled, the voices of Sue and Tanya quiet beyond the plaster walls. They had spent over an hour going over their recordings from their last session at Menlo Lab, but they had only confirmed what they already knew. Now, they were asleep—everyone except Ellen.

She stared at the blank page for what felt like hours.

Her charcoal pencil sat poised between her fingers, waiting. But nothing came. Not a line. Not a whisper. Only the soft ticking of the antique clock on the nightstand and the occasional rattle of leaves outside.

Ellen exhaled through her nose. "Come on, Edison," she whispered. "You said you'd help us. So, help me. Please. Show me what you want us to build."

She adjusted her posture, cross-legged now, and let her shoulders relax. She'd done this before. Opened herself to the strange frequency that allowed spirits to guide her hand. It wasn't something she controlled exactly—it came when it came, like a tide.

She let her eyes unfocus, her mind empty. Let her thoughts fall away.

And then her hand moved.

At first, it was just a back-and-forth line, like idle doodling. She didn't look down. That was part of the process. No expectations. Just let it flow. Her pencil scratched softly over the page. She wasn't aware of her breathing. Wasn't aware of the room. Only the strange rhythm of charcoal against paper, like a slow dance guided by invisible fingers.

She wasn't sure how long she had drifted—minutes, maybe more.

Then something shifted. Her spine gave a little jolt, her eyes blinked fully open, and she looked down.

The page was no longer blank.

Her breath caught in her throat.

Drawn in meticulous, almost mechanical precision, was something that resembled a handheld electric drill—but *not quite*. It had an oblong handle with strange wire spiraling along the shaft, and a chamber that looked like it held some kind of crystal. What she assumed was the "bit" of the device wasn't a drill at all, but a coil-shaped extension that flared into something resembling the mouth of a gramophone. The whole apparatus looked like it was meant to channel or *emit* something rather than puncture.

Ellen touched the edges of the page. Her fingers trembled.

It was beautiful and bizarre—part steampunk, part science fiction. She hadn't designed this. Not consciously. She knew her own drawing style: loose, expressive, intuitive. But this was almost architectural. Rendered in tight, deliberate lines with shaded cross-sections, it looked like a patent diagram. The device floated on the page, annotated with little arrows and circles, though no words. No labels.

"Good grief," she whispered. "What are we supposed to do with *this*?"

A strange ache settled between her shoulder blades. She wanted to feel accomplished—grateful, even. After all, Edison had answered her plea. He'd shown her what they needed.

But instead, she felt stumped. Frustrated. A little afraid.

How were they supposed to build this? What materials did it need? How did it work? It looked like something out of a fever dream—ingenious but alien. She and her friends weren't electrical engineers, after all. Tanya had a solid mind for assembling things like IKEA furniture, but even she would need a manual, or at least a list of parts. Sue would try to research it, Ellen knew, but there was nothing like this in any book.

She stared at the page a moment longer, searching for meaning. But none came.

With a sigh, she closed the sketchbook and set it gently on the nightstand beside the lamp. The room felt colder now. More hollow. The trance had drained her, left her empty in that way that always followed spirit contact—like waking from a vivid dream and realizing the world had moved on without you.

Ellen slid back under the quilt, pulling it up to her chin.

She closed her eyes.

"Please," she said aloud, "if you're still listening, Thomas Alva Edison, I need more than a sketch. We need instructions. We need you to show us how. Not just the what. The how."

The shadows in the corners of the room didn't answer.

She lay there listening to the old house breathe, to the wind curling past the glass, wondering what waited for them at the windmill. What would happen if they couldn't figure it out in time?

Eventually, her thoughts slowed. The warmth of the bed crept into her bones.

And just before sleep took her, a final thought echoed through her mind—not her own, not entirely:

The answer is already written. You just haven't seen it yet.

Ellen stood in the middle of Menlo Lab, but it wasn't how she remembered it. Everything shimmered, faintly translucent, as though she was walking through the memory of a place rather than the place itself. A low hum vibrated in the air, deep and electric, like standing too close to a substation. The overhead lights flickered with a sickly, amber glow.

She turned slowly in place. Shadows danced behind frosted windows, and old machines seemed to pulse with life.

"Hello?" she called out.

No answer came.

Then—footsteps. Slow, even. From the far end of the lab, past a display of glass vacuum tubes and dusty workbenches, a figure emerged.

It was the Hat Man.

But this time, he appeared to her as more than a shadowy silhouette. He wore a dark waistcoat and a gray felt hat. His expression was calm and studious.

"Thomas Alva Edison?" Ellen asked, her voice catching.

He nodded once.

Without speaking, he raised his hand and gestured toward a nearby table. On it lay a strange collection of mismatched objects: a bright red plastic water gun, its nozzle cracked; a length of coiled copper wire; a flickering, half-shattered light bulb; two bulky batteries; a handful of metal screws; a silver fishing reel; a curved sewing needle; a quartz crystal; and what looked like a rubber gasket from a garden hose.

"These are the parts," he said finally, his voice clear but echoing strangely. "Each is important."

Ellen stared at them, puzzled—until, slowly, her mind began piecing them together like components of a puzzle. It wasn't just junk. *These could form the body of the device.* Housing, wiring, a power source, and some kind of rudimentary motor. It was crude. Makeshift. But possible.

Ellen took a step forward, staring at the collection.

Edison moved aside, revealing another table, empty except for a sheet of aged paper. As she watched, ink began to materialize across its surface. Schematics. The same image she'd sketched earlier, but now overlaid with numbers, symbols, and a series of small notations in an elegant, slanted hand.

His hand.

Then the vision began to blur. The lab darkened.

Ellen's heart raced. "Wait! I don't understand—what are we supposed to—"

Edison looked at her again. "The instructions are on the pages I told Charles to burn. The end of the journal. After the goodbye."

He raised a finger and pointed to the ceiling. Ellen followed his gaze.

Above them, a windmill spun slowly—upside down—its blades turning against a moonless sky.

And then she awoke.

For a moment, Ellen didn't move. Her heart was still galloping from the dream, her body too warm under the blankets. It had been *so vivid*. The copper wire, the water gun, batteries, the voice of Edison in her head.

She sat up slowly and rubbed her face. Then she reached for the sketchbook on the nightstand and opened to the page she'd drawn the night before.

The device was still there—detailed, mechanical, impossible.

A knock sounded softly on her door.

"Ellen?" Tanya's voice, slightly groggy. "Bagels and caffeine in the kitchen."

"Be right there."

She dressed quickly and padded barefoot downstairs, the creaky steps making her feel like a teenager sneaking in after curfew. The scent of dark roast coffee and toasted sesame bagels greeted her as she stepped into the cozy, colonial-style kitchen. Sunlight pooled across the wide pine floors, and Sue was already at the long table, cream cheese in one hand, her reading glasses perched at the end of her nose.

"You look like you saw a ghost," Sue said with a smirk.

Ellen gave a tired smile. "I didn't see him." She set the sketchbook down on the table, opened to her most recent drawing. "But he did this."

Tanya turned from the coffeepot, interest sparking in her eyes. "Did you draw that?"

"I was in a trance. I didn't know what I was drawing until it was finished."

Tanya leaned over the image, her brows lifting. "That's incredible. It's like a handheld generator crossed with a Tesla coil."

"That's not all." Ellen looked between them. "I dreamed I was back in Menlo Lab. Edison was there. He showed me this table full of strange items—things we're supposed to collect. I think they're materials for the device."

Sue lowered her bagel. "I had the same dream. Almost exactly. A water gun and fishing reel—I thought it was just some bizarre subconscious metaphor."

"Same here," Tanya said. "Except mine ended with something else—He said the instructions are written there now. At the end. Past the letter to Charles."

Ellen's mouth fell open slightly. "He told *me* the same thing."

"Me, too," Sue said, standing up to grab her phone. "Where's the journal?"

Ellen hastened to the sitting room and retrieved Edison's secret journal from one of her bags. She carried it to a wide side table beneath the kitchen window and opened to the last entry—the one Edison had written to his son, Charles, confessing his smear campaign against Westinghouse and Tesla.

Sue and Tanya gathered around her, holding their breath.

Beyond the closing signature—*Your father, Thomas Alva Edison*—the pages appeared untouched. Off-white. Pristine.

And then . . . a spark.

The ink shimmered, faint at first, like an incandescent bulb turning on. A single line appeared, like the stroke of a fountain pen moving across paper.

You must build it exactly as described. No substitutions. No deviations.

The words were followed by an intricate diagram—far more detailed than Ellen's trance sketch. It was the same device, but broken into labeled sections, each with notes in Edison's unmistakable hand. Descriptions of the parts: the copper coil wound around the core; the adapted water gun housing; the battery chamber; the configuration of the fishing reel motor; how the sewing needle must be aligned with the quartz crystal.

As they watched, more lines appeared—step-by-step instructions, calculations, material ratios.

Tanya paled. "That wasn't there before."

"I know," Ellen said softly. Her voice trembled, though she tried to steady it. "He's still working. Even now."

Tanya ran a hand over her mouth, staring as if the pages might burst into flames. "I guess this will help us to stop the windmill from whispering, to close the portal."

"Yes," Sue said. "If we survive."

"We'll survive," Ellen assured her friends, though she wasn't so sure herself.

CHAPTER TWENTY-THREE

If You Build It

The automatic doors whooshed open, releasing a burst of chilled air that smelled faintly of plastic and disinfectant. Ellen stepped into Walmart with her two closest friends on either side, the fluorescent lights buzzing overhead like discontented bees.

Behind them, C.W. pushed an empty cart with the solemnity of a chauffeur navigating unfamiliar terrain.

"Well," Sue said, glancing down at the hastily scribbled list, "let's go gather the arcane ingredients of our ghost-busting spell, shall we?"

"I'll take the batteries and light bulbs," Tanya offered, already veering toward electronics.

"I'll get the toy section," Ellen said. "You know, where all the magical portal-closing water guns are kept."

C.W. gave her a mock salute. "I'll go find snacks. No way you're saving the world without gummy worms."

"I like the way you think," Sue said to C.W. "I guess I'll look for the rest of the materials, starting with the curved sewing needle."

They split up, navigating the aisles like seasoned treasure hunters. Ellen found the water guns quickly—a neon-green Super Soaker with a cracked cap caught her eye. It looked ridiculous, but in her mind, she could already see it housing the copper coil and batteries. She picked it up with the solemnity of someone choosing a weapon from a sacred armory.

By the time they regrouped near checkout, they had everything but the copper wire and the quartz crystal.

"Hardware store next?" Sue asked.

"On Ford Road," C.W. said, pulling out his phone. "Eight minutes, give or take traffic delays."

The hardware store was nearly empty when they arrived, the bell on the door chiming softly. Ellen trailed a finger along rows of screws and wire spools, befuddled by gauges and tensile strength. They found the perfect roll—bright copper, flexible but strong.

After they paid and left the store, C.W. loaded the bag with the rest in the back of his car. "Y'all building a bomb or a time machine?"

Ellen smiled. "Neither. Just a way to close the gates of the underworld."

He blinked. "Well, I hope it comes with instructions."

Sue muttered, "Sort of."

"Next stop," Tanya turned to C.W., "crystal shop."

The sun was already sinking as they returned to the Patrick Henry House. Shadows stretched long across the garden, and cicadas buzzed in the background like nature's static. Ellen carried the bag with the journal like it might detonate if jostled.

C.W. helped them unload the gear onto the long dining table, then hesitated at the door.

"You sure you don't want help? I do know how to use a screwdriver."

"Thanks," Sue said, giving his hand a squeeze. "But we've got this."

"At least, we hope we do," Tanya murmured.

C.W. held Sue's gaze a moment longer, and Ellen wondered if maybe he really *was* into Sue. Then, he nodded. "Okay. But call if the thing starts smoking or growling."

As the door closed behind him, Ellen exhaled and set the water gun down in the center of the table. Tanya flicked on the chandelier light overhead, and Sue passed out bottles of water like they were gearing up for a marathon.

"So, we gut it first?" Tanya asked, rolling up her sleeves.

Ellen nodded. "I'll do the dissection. Someone read the schematics again."

Sue opened the journal to the final pages. The writing had stopped manifesting, but the diagrams and instructions were clear. They laid out the order in which parts should be placed, how the coil should be wrapped, and how the batteries needed to be seated to conduct a low, continuous current—strong enough to interact with spiritual energy, but not strong enough to electrocute anyone living.

As Ellen carefully dismantled the water gun, she marveled at how perfectly the shape fit the device in her sketch. Tanya had already wound the copper wire into the correct configuration, checking the coil against Edison's diagram with almost obsessive precision.

They worked for an hour in relative silence, save for the occasional burst of colorful language from Tanya when the screws didn't line up.

They didn't eat so much as inhale their DoorDash pasta, alternating bites of penne and swigs of water while assembling and soldering.

"Who knew building a ghost drill would be the weirdest thing we did this week?" Sue muttered, pointing her headband light toward the device while Ellen soldered the wire ends to the terminals of the batteries.

"Speak for yourself," Ellen said. "I got goosed by Henry Ford's ghost."

"Really?" Tanya asked with lifted brows.

Ellen shook her head. "You're too easy, Tanya."

They all laughed—until Sue's phone buzzed loudly on the table.

Sue glanced at the screen. "It's John."

Ellen and Tanya looked up at once.

"Put him on speaker," Ellen said.

Sue tapped a button. "John? We're—"

"Things have gotten worse," John's voice interrupted, tense and low. "My staff's reporting incidents."

"What kind of incidents?" Tanya asked sharply.

"I thought it was a prank at first. One of the night guards said he saw someone on the Greenfield Village grounds. He gave chase. Said it looked like a teenager."

Ellen felt her stomach tighten. "And?"

"He *ran through* him," John said. "Said the air went cold. Then the kid just disappeared. And he's not the only one. Someone saw a figure near the Menlo Lab window. Another near the covered bridge. They're all seeing different people—some dressed like it's 1920, others in rags."

Sue glanced at Ellen, then Tanya. "They're coming through."

"Yes," John confirmed. "I think the portal's widening. And there's something else."

Ellen held her breath.

"What is it, John?" Sue prompted.

"It could be a coincidence, but Leroy . . . you met him, he was one of my docents at Menlo Park . . . was found dead in Menlo Lab early this morning."

Ellen felt the blood leave her face. She glanced at her friends, who had turned as pale as she had.

"No known cause of death?" Ellen managed to ask.

"They're saying heart attack, but I don't know, ladies. I'm worried that it may have had something to do with the windmill."

"We're on it," Ellen assured him once her wits had returned. She told him about the device they were building and their plan to return to the windmill to use it. That very night.

"Sounds terrifying," John admitted. "Call me when you're ready to head up there."

The line went dead.

No one moved for a long moment.

Then Sue clapped her hands. "All right, let's build this thing."

They got back to work, this time with urgency. The rubber gasket was fitted around the wire chamber, the fishing reel affixed to the internal motor unit, the batteries nestled snugly into their slots. Lastly, the crystal went into its cavity before Ellen attached the sewing needle, threading it through a channel Tanya had melted into the plastic body with a hot butter knife. It looked almost surgical.

When the last screw clicked into place, they all stood back and stared.

The device was ugly—a Frankenstein of salvaged parts and historical desperation—but it pulsed faintly with a heat that seemed both electric and otherworldly.

"It's humming," Sue whispered.

"Like it's alive," Tanya added.

Ellen picked it up. It vibrated faintly in her hand, like it was aware. A low, steady thrum passed through her palm, up her arm, into her shoulder. It wasn't painful—just *present.*

"I think it's working," she said.

Outside, the wind picked up.

Inside, Ellen glanced once more at the open journal on the table. The final page remained still . . . until, as if ink were seeping up from beneath the paper, a new line began to form beneath the instructions.

Sue leaned in. "It's happening again."

The sentence emerged slowly, deliberate and shaking, as if written by an unsteady hand on the other side of the veil.

Return to the windmill before the moon reaches its peak.

Ellen's breath caught in her throat. Then, a second line appeared, just beneath it.

And take with you a tether to the living.

Sue read it aloud, frowning. "'A tether to the living'? What does that mean?"

As if in answer, another sentence bloomed across the page.

You will see the dead. Some will be known to you. They may tempt you to stay. You need a reason to return.

Tanya exhaled sharply. "Well, that's horrifying."

"Edison's warning us," Ellen said softly. "That we might see people we've lost. People we miss."

Sue reached for the edge of the table to steady herself. "That's cruel. What if I see my mother?"

Tanya looked pale. "If I see my parents, I'll fall apart."

Ellen swallowed hard, thinking of Paul, gone for nearly five years. What if she could feel his arms around her once more? Could she leave him again?

But Edison was right—they had to come back. She wanted to come back. Her children, her grandchildren, Brian.

"A tethering object," Ellen said, more to herself than anyone. "Something from the living. Something that reminds us we belong here."

They each went quiet.

"I've got just the thing," Sue said suddenly. She pulled out her wallet and flipped it open to a small photo tucked behind her insurance card—Lexi and Stephen with Shep and Lily in front of a swimming pool, soaked and happy. "This'll do."

Tanya ran upstairs. She returned a minute later clutching a silver locket. "Mike gave me this when he moved to Austin," she said, opening it. Inside were two tiny portraits, barely the size of thumbnails. "Camie on one side, Mike on the other. My tethers."

Ellen realized she was wearing her tethering object—a bracelet Brian had given her for their anniversary last year. It was silver with turquoise beads, handcrafted in Santa Fe.

She twirled it around her wrist, the cool weight oddly comforting. "I'm ready."

When they reconvened in the hallway, bundled into coats and clinging to their objects like lifelines, Ellen took one last glance around the Patrick Henry House. The warm glow of the reading lamps. The dented throw pillow from Tanya's back. The empty teacups on the counter. A quiet stillness filled the house, as if it, too, was anxious.

Outside, the moon had risen higher, haloed in a misty ring. Time was slipping.

Sue tapped her phone. "Calling John now."

He picked up instantly. "You're ready?"

"We are. Meet us at the curb."

"On my way."

By the time they stepped out into the night, John's Ford Explorer was already waiting, headlights cutting through the soft fog rolling off the lawn. He stood outside the driver's door, arms folded, face drawn.

"You ready for this?" he asked.

Ellen nodded. "It's why we came."

John looked from one to the other, seeming to understand more than he said. "Then let's not waste another second."

He opened the back door.

Ellen and Sue climbed in without a word as Tanya, carrying the bag with the device, climbed in front.

Behind them, the Patrick Henry House stood silent, bathed in silver moonlight.

Ahead of them, the windmill waited.

CHAPTER TWENTY-FOUR

Journey to the Center of the Portal

The wrought-iron gates of Greenfield Village creaked open under the mechanical protest of old hinges, their groans lost in the hush of the late-night hour. John Coleman stood beside the entrance, flashlight in hand, his face pale under the lamppost overhead. The wind was cool and damp, carrying the scent of cut grass and something older—earthier. Ellen stepped through the gates, the Frankenstein device cradled in her arms like a colicky baby. Tanya followed, fingering her locket, while Sue clutched the photo of Lexi's family. Ellen touched Brian's bracelet nervously.

Of course, she and her friends would return from the portal. Why wouldn't they?

"You sure you don't want to come with us?" Sue asked John as he closed the gate behind them.

John shook his head. "I've done a lot of things for the museum, but this is something else. I'll be right here. If you're not back in an hour, I'm calling everyone. Police. Press. Priest."

Ellen managed a grim smile. "Let's hope we don't need any of them."

They walked in silence through the sleeping village, past the now-familiar silhouettes of antique homes, picket fences, and lampposts. The moon hadn't yet reached its peak, but its silvery glow bathed the path ahead. With each step, Ellen felt the bracelet around her wrist shift gently against her skin. It was a small tether in the growing unreality of the moment.

"Do you hear that?" Tanya asked, her voice low.

At first, Ellen thought she meant the whispers—ever-present at the windmill—but then she heard it too: footsteps, dragging slightly, coming from somewhere behind the old general store.

A woman emerged. She appeared no older than thirty, in a pale linen dress that fluttered in the breeze, her eyes wide and darting. She held out her hands.

"Clara?" she cried. "Where is Clara? What have you done with her?"

The three friends froze. The ghost's presence was not subtle. Ellen could see the glimmering edges of her form, semi-transparent, yet startlingly vivid.

"We—we don't know Clara," Ellen said gently, backing up a step. "We're sorry."

"She was just here!" The woman's tone sharpened with panic. "She went to the mill—she *followed the voice!*" Her form shimmered violently, as though barely holding together. "Bring her back!"

Before any of them could answer, a soft shuffle of movement caught their attention from the opposite direction. Another spirit was approaching, older, bent at the spine, wearing suspenders and dust-covered boots. His eyes were clouded with confusion.

"Mary?" he croaked. "Have you seen my Mary?"

"We haven't," Tanya said, inching closer to Ellen. "I'm sorry. We can't help."

"Everyone's looking," the man murmured, half to himself.

The whispers intensified. The wind picked up, curling around their ankles like tendrils. The ghosts flickered once—twice—then vanished with a sudden, unnatural silence.

"We need to move," Sue said, already striding ahead.

The windmill loomed ahead like a giant skeleton, its blades gently moving against the moonlit sky. The whispering had grown louder, as though the structure itself was exhaling in a language not meant for living ears.

Together, they approached the base of the windmill and pulled open the wooden door. The air inside was thick with mildew and static. The stairs spiraled upward in the narrow shaft, worn from decades—centuries—of use. They stepped in, gripping each other's hands, afraid of what came next.

The stairs creaked under their feet as they ascended. The higher they climbed, the louder the whispering became. Not all of it was in English—or if it was, it had been so warped by time and distance that it had become something entirely different. Ellen squeezed Tanya's hand and tightened her grip on the device. Her bracelet pressed against her wrist.

At the top, the cramped room beneath the windmill's cap waited like a hollow crown. The floor was bare. The wind spun lazily through cracks in the walls, tugging at their clothes and hair.

"So now what?" Sue asked, her voice barely audible over the whisper-storm.

Ellen glanced around, searching for anything—an object, a sign, a shimmer of ghostly light. "Thomas Alva Edison?" she called out. "Are you here?" She raised the device, which buzzed in her hand. "We have the machine. We followed your instructions. What now?"

Nothing. Only the deep, rhythmic creak of the windmill's timbers and the ever-present whispering.

"We're missing something," Tanya said.

Ellen stared at the device—its mismatched parts, the absurdity of it. They were standing in a windmill trying to close a portal to the dead, and she was holding what looked like a possessed water gun.

Her skin prickled.

"Or maybe," Ellen murmured, "this *is* it. Maybe we just have to want to cross to the other side. Try focusing on that."

They stood there, hand in hand, focusing, waiting for the next sign, as the moon slid higher in the sky behind them.

The air in the windmill's crown shifted, charged with something more than atmosphere—a pulling sensation, subtle but unmistakable. Ellen felt it in her chest, like a thread tightening around her heart. The device in her hand gave a sudden, jerky thrum.

"It's working," Ellen whispered.

Then, the world around them shimmered.

The wooden walls of the windmill dissolved into haze. Everything turned white with a brightness that didn't blind but enveloped. For a breathless moment, Ellen could see nothing but light. Then, shapes began to form—trees with no visible roots, a stream that whispered instead of burbled, a field of soft, violet grass stretching beyond reason, and people—so many people!

She turned to Tanya and Sue, who stood beside her, eyes wide. The device hung loose in Ellen's hand. Her bracelet felt oddly heavier, pulling against her wrist like an anchor.

"Looks like we're in," Tanya said hesitantly.

Before anyone could reply, two figures walked slowly toward them.

Tanya gasped, stepping forward. "Mom? Dad?"

The couple approached with familiar smiles. Tanya's mother had short, white hair and soft, apple-round cheeks. Her father's posture was just as Ellen remembered: proud, despite the slight stoop of age. Without a word, Tanya rushed into their embrace. Her shoulders shook with silent sobs.

"Oh, sweetheart," her mother murmured, brushing a strand of hair from Tanya's face. "We've been watching. We're so proud of you—but you shouldn't be here."

"You're not safe," her father added gently.

Tanya held onto them like she never wanted to let go. Ellen felt tears sting her own eyes. She remembered Tanya losing them both in the same year that Ellen lost her own mother. To see Tanya with them now made Ellen ache with a mixture of joy and sadness.

But before she could speak, another voice cut through the mist.

"You never call, you never write," came a familiar, sarcastic tone. "I was beginning to think you forgot me entirely. And did you re-member to put on deodorant this morning?"

Sue let out a shocked laugh as Jan, her mother, strode into view, hands on her hips, her smile full of mischief.

"Mom!" Sue burst out, running forward. "Gawd, I've missed you."

"Believe it or not, I've actually missed you, too," Jan said, softening. She folded Sue into her arms as her daughter wept.

Ellen approached more slowly, smiling through her own tears. "Hi, Jan. You haven't changed a bit."

"That's the benefit of being dead," Jan said with a wink. "No wrinkles."

They all laughed, though the air felt too full of emotion for it to last. Ellen glanced at Tanya, still huddled in her parents' arms, and at Sue, leaning into her mother, and felt warmth bloom in her chest.

She glanced around the many souls in the mist, wondering if she'd see her own parents.

And then she saw him.

Paul.

He stood a little distance away, his expression unsure, hopeful. He looked just as she remembered from their final years together: slightly graying at the temples, laugh lines around his mouth, that same lopsided smile that used to melt her anger in an instant.

Ellen's heart slammed in her chest. The device slipped from her hand, landing softly in the grass.

"Paul!" she cried, rushing toward him.

He opened his arms and caught her in a tight embrace. She pressed her face against his shoulder, breathing in his scent as the memories of him flooded her.

"I missed you so much," she murmured.

"I know," he whispered. "Me too. How are the kids?"

Ellen pulled back just enough to see his face. "Nolan's back in San Antonio at North Central Baptist Hospital. He was born there, remember? He's married to Taylor—you met her once, didn't you? They have two children—Brianna and Mason. Lane's married, too, to a sweet girl named Maya. A Vanderbilt!"

"Ah, so he can afford to make his art then, huh?" Paul asked with a laugh.

Tears flooded Ellen's eyes as she nodded. "You'd love her. They have a son named Travis. Alison is working at a hospital in Austin. She loves being a radiographer. She likes the dark room and the quiet."

Paul's smile widened. "I check on them from time to time. They look happy."

She wondered if he ever checked on her, too. "They miss you."

He gave her a solemn smile.

She looked into his eyes. "I don't know what made me think of this, but do you remember Nolan's first scout camp, when he had to stand in front of the group gathered around the bonfire and tell a joke?"

Paul laughed. "The one about the ghost who got kicked out of the haunted house for being too scared? He made it up on the spot!"

"And everyone laughed so hard. He was so proud." Back then, Ellen didn't believe in ghosts. Who knew Nolan's joke would be so relevant to her today?

They stood together, wrapped in memory. Time seemed suspended. The longer Ellen stood with Paul, the less she remembered why they'd come. Something about the portal. Something about a device. But Paul was here. He felt *real*. Her tether—the bracelet on her wrist—pressed tighter against her skin, but even that sensation was fading.

"I could stay," Ellen said softly. "We could have more time. There's so much I want to tell you." She looked back briefly toward Sue and Tanya, who were still with their families. Everything about this place felt peaceful, warm. "Would it be wrong?" she asked. "To stay?"

Paul didn't answer. His smile was wistful, full of sadness and longing.

She leaned into him again, letting her eyes close.

The bracelet pulsed. Not a real pulse, but a phantom one—like her wrist remembering its weight. A reminder. Brian. Their new life. Her children and grandchildren, still among the living.

But wasn't Paul worth staying for?

And yet, hadn't she spent three decades by his side already?

But the thought of leaving him again crushed her.

"Ellen," he said gently, pulling away. "You need to go back."

She turned, looking at where the device had fallen. It lay in the grass, inert.

Would it still work?

Did she care?

She took a step toward it—then stopped and turned to Paul.

Paul backed away from her. "Please, as much as I want you to stay, you must go back."

Ellen hesitated.

The wind moaned low through the grass as Ellen wandered farther from Paul, the mist parting reluctantly around her. She barely registered her own breathing, her fingers clenching and unclenching at her sides as a strange sense of wrongness returned, seeping into her bones. Something pulled at her memory, something urgent—something about a device. A mission.

Then, from the swirling fog behind her, a shout sliced through the stillness.

"Where do you think you're going?"

Ellen turned. George Flint stumbled into view, disheveled and wild-eyed, dragging one foot like he'd twisted his ankle. His jacket was torn, his glasses cracked, but the fury in his expression was unmistakable.

"George?" Ellen gasped, taking a step back. "How did you—?"

"Out on bond," he growled, catching his breath. "And John Coleman? Out cold by the gate. You think I didn't know you'd come back here eventually? I've been waiting. This is my last chance. You can't shut it down. I won't let you."

He staggered closer, eyes darting behind her. A strange light shone in them—not rage now, but longing. "They're here. My wife . . . my daughter. I can see them again, whenever I please!"

Before Ellen could respond, the mist parted, and two figures emerged from the crowd of wandering souls: a woman with kind eyes and a younger woman holding her hand. George let out a sound that was half sob, half laughter. He rushed to them and fell to his knees, clutching them close.

Ellen's heart clenched. The tenderness in his voice, the way he cradled them—it was love, unfiltered and raw. And for a moment, she faltered. Maybe they didn't have to shut the portal. Maybe people *should* be allowed to see their loved ones again.

She glanced over her shoulder. Paul stood a few feet away, holding something in his hand.

The device.

He stepped forward and gently placed it in her hand. "Ellen," he said, voice low and calm, "you have to do the right thing."

"What if it traps us here?" she whispered, her grip tightening around the strange, Frankensteinian machine. "Maybe that's okay."

Paul looked past her. "Call out to them. Remind them that you have to go back."

She trembled. The pull of Paul's presence, the possibility of staying, was so strong it made her dizzy.

"I don't know what I'm supposed to do or how to get back to the windmill," she admitted. "I don't even know how this thing works! Thomas Alva Edison! Help me! What do I do next?"

A figure stepped out of the misty crowd.

The Hat Man.

Once again, he was not a faceless shadow. The outline was clear now, and so was the face—the wizard of Menlo Park, in his prime. Deep-set blue-green eyes, sharp with purpose.

He held out his hand.

Without hesitation, Ellen gave him the device.

"Thank you for all you've done," he said kindly. He handed the device to Paul. "I need one more favor. Count to twenty and then pull the trigger to keep both realms safe." Edison turned to Ellen. "We've got to go. Now!"

Ellen glanced once more at her beloved Paul, her heart aching for him. Would he pull the trigger in time?

"Go!" Paul shouted at her.

Before she could think more about it, Ellen turned and ran, following Thomas Edison through the mist.

"Sue! Tanya!" she cried, dashing through the tall grass and spectral haze. "We have to go! Now! Follow us!"

She found Sue standing beside her mother, tears staining her cheeks, Jan's hands on her shoulders. Nearby, Tanya stood between her parents, her face buried in her father's chest.

"You have to come with us," Ellen said, breathless. "The portal—it's closing. We need to leave."

"But—" Tanya started, her eyes wide and wet.

"Look at your tether," Edison insisted. "That's why you brought them. To remember."

Sue blinked and looked at the photo still clutched in her hand, as if seeing it for the first time. Tanya opened the locket hanging around her neck. Bit by bit, the spell broke.

"There's no more time, ladies!" Edison warned. "Follow me!"

The three friends linked hands and began to run after Edison. Behind them, George shouted something.

"George!" Ellen glanced back and saw him kneeling, arms wrapped around his wife and daughter. "We have to go! Now!"

"You go!" he yelled. "Leave me!"

The windmill emerged from the fog like a ghostly guardian. The moon, massive and silver, was cresting its peak above them.

"Hurry!" Edison's voice rang out.

They sprinted the last few steps, burst through the door, and scrambled up the creaking stairs. A blinding, white light surged through the windmill tower. The air crackled with energy.

The floorboards trembled beneath their feet.

The light engulfed them.

And then—

Silence.

Ellen opened her eyes. They were still standing inside the windmill, the old floorboards beneath their feet, the night cool against their flushed faces. The moon hung high in the sky, still and bright.

But there was no more whispering, no more engulfing light. No more Edison.

Sue was the first to speak. "Is it over?"

"Did we do it?" Tanya asked. "Did it work?"

Ellen looked through the tower window. No figures wandering in a mist. No whispering voices riding the wind. The air felt quiet. Still.

"Where's George?" Ellen asked.

No one answered.

Then Ellen's eyes widened. "John! George said he knocked John out!"

The three of them bolted down the steps and exited the windmill, feet pounding against the ground as they raced for the entrance to Greenfield Village.

John lay sprawled beside the iron gate, unmoving.

Ellen bent over him. "John! Can you hear me?"

Sue pressed her fingers to his neck. "He's got a pulse. He's still breathing."

Tanya whipped out her phone and tapped it. "I'm calling 9-1-1."

They hovered over him, the portal behind them now silent and—hopefully—closed. But as the ambulance sirens wailed in the distance, none of them knew for certain if the dead that had previously escaped were trapped over here, just as George Flint was trapped over there.

Ellen clutched the bracelet on her wrist, heart aching as Paul's face flooded her mind. No sooner had she thought of him than she saw two ghosts wandering the streets of the park.

She glanced at her friends, and the looks on their faces told her that they were the were thinking the same thing: This wasn't over.

CHAPTER TWENTY-FIVE

The Morning After

Fluorescent lights buzzed overhead in the sterile hospital corridor, and an antiseptic scent lingered in the air. Ellen stood just outside the open door to Room 213, her arms crossed and her heart heavy. John Coleman lay unmoving in the hospital bed, his face pale against the starched white sheets, machines clicking and humming softly around him. His wife, a woman in her late forties with long, dark hair and a trembling jaw, sat beside him clutching his hand. Their son, who appeared to be in his mid-twenties, stood at the foot of the bed, lips pressed into a tight line, blinking back tears.

No one spoke.

Sue touched Ellen's arm gently. "We should give them some space."

Ellen nodded, grateful. "Yeah. And I'm beat."

Tanya trailed behind them as they made their way down the long hallway, their footsteps muffled by the linoleum.

"Poor John," Tanya murmured. "I can't believe Flint did this to him."

"The man's a coward," Sue said, her voice low but firm. "I don't care how sad his life was. Using force and manipulation to get what he wants was just wrong."

Ellen sighed. "And now John's paying the price."

"What if he never wakes from his coma?" Tanya murmured.

"We have to believe he will," Sue replied.

They found a waiting area near the entrance with a small bank of vending machines and a view of the parking lot through tinted windows. Ellen sank into one of the vinyl chairs.

"So," Tanya asked, after a moment of silence. "Do we just go back to the Patrick Henry House?"

"We should," Ellen said. "We all need rest."

"It's probably too late to call C.W.," Tanya said, already pulling out her phone.

Sue glanced at the time on her phone. "It's after midnight. I think we should let him sleep. Just book an Uber."

Tanya sighed, tapped her screen, and said, "All right. Blue Ford Expedition. ETA: six minutes."

They headed to the curb, stepping into the chilly night. The crisp air held a faint smell of damp pavement. Somewhere in the distance, a siren wailed, then faded.

"That place," Sue said, breaking the silence. "The portal. I can't stop thinking about it."

"Same," Tanya agreed. "It was like stepping into a memory you didn't want to end."

Ellen nodded, her hands deep in her coat pockets. "Seeing Paul again . . . It was the hardest and most beautiful thing that's happened to me in years."

"I still can't believe my mom cracked that deodorant joke from beyond the grave," Sue said, her voice thick. She laughed softly and wiped at her eyes. "Only she could make me cry and laugh at the same time."

Tanya's voice trembled. "I keep hearing my mom's voice. Telling me she was proud of me. I don't want to forget it."

Ellen looked at them both, her chest tightening. "We won't forget. That's the gift. We got to see them one more time, and we came back—though I have to admit, I was really tempted to stay. Weren't you?"

Sue and Tanya exchanged glances before offering solemn nods.

"I wonder why I didn't see my parents," Ellen suddenly said.

"I didn't see my dad," Sue pointed out.

Tanya shrugged. "Maybe we saw the people we think about the most."

A vehicle pulled up, headlights flashing briefly. The blue Ford Expedition rolled to a stop, and the window came down.

"Hey there, ladies! You headed to the Patrick Henry House?"

The driver was a cheerful woman with curly, brown hair pulled back into a ponytail and large hoop earrings. She had a warm smile and a sparkly steering wheel cover.

"That's us," Sue replied before opening the back door.

They climbed in, and the woman adjusted the music volume, soft jazz playing in the background.

"Long night?"

"You could say that," Ellen replied.

Sue and Tanya giggled.

As they continued toward Dearborn Inn, Sue whispered, "She's nice enough, but she's no C.W."

Ellen lay in bed in her upstairs bedroom at the Patrick Henry House, the room dim except for the halo of moonlight peeking through the slit between the curtains. Sleep had eluded her so far. The events of the last twenty-four hours reeled through her mind like a jittery film projector. Her muscles ached with exhaustion, and her spirit felt threadbare. She clutched the edge of the quilt and pulled it up to her chin.

Paul's face hovered in her thoughts—his familiar smile, the sound of his laugh, the way his eyes crinkled when he teased her. Being with him in the spirit realm had been both heartwarming and devastating. There was no question she'd loved him deeply. They'd built a life together. Raised children. Weathered grief. Shared joy. His death had carved out a hollow in her heart that had never truly closed.

But now there was Brian. Sweet, patient Brian, who knew how to make her laugh even when she didn't feel like laughing. Who brought her coffee just the way she liked it. Who encouraged her art, her ghost-healing, her entire self. They had a different kind of love—not rooted in youth or early ambition, but in the comfort of knowing, and being known. With Brian, there was still growth. Still adventures to be had. She hadn't expected that.

Tears slid silently down the sides of her face and into her hair. She wiped them away with the edge of the sheet. What if she hadn't come back from the portal? What if she'd stayed with Paul, lulled by the ache of nostalgia and love? Her children would've been devastated. They'd already lost one parent. And what about Brian? His bracelet on the nightstand now pulsed with a kind of emotional weight, grounding her in the present.

She turned over to stare at the bracelet, pulling the quilt close, and thought about last Christmas, when everyone was together at her house. Even her brother Jody and his family had come.

She wasn't stuck in the past. She was lucky enough to love and be loved again. To be alive. And she was doing something that mattered. Something that made her feel useful and brave and uniquely herself.

Down the hall, she heard the soft creak of floorboards. Maybe Sue or Tanya couldn't sleep either. Maybe they were also wrestling with the pull of old ghosts and the blessings of their present lives. It was no wonder that portal had affected them so deeply.

Ellen closed her eyes and took a long, slow breath. She would tell Brian everything when she got home. About Paul. About the portal. About what she felt, and what she chose. He would understand. She wasn't sure what she and her team would do about the other ghosts still trapped on this side—Charles McElvaine and the others—but Brian's support and understanding? Of that, she was certain.

Thursday morning, the scent of fresh coffee greeted Ellen as she padded into the kitchen in her slippers. Sue was already at the counter, spreading cream cheese on a toasted bagel. Tanya stood by the window, peering out at the sun rising over the manicured lawn.

"Good morning," Ellen said, her voice still hoarse with sleep.

Sue glanced over her shoulder. "Hey. How'd you sleep?"

"Like a rock once I finally let go of everything." Ellen moved toward the coffee pot, pouring herself a steaming cup.

Tanya turned, her eyes soft but focused. "I kept dreaming about the portal. Like we left something undone."

Ellen took a sip and nodded. "We did, in a way. There are spirits that may still be trapped on this side—especially Charles McElvaine."

Sue raised an eyebrow. "True. We need a plan. I'm anxious to get out of here."

"Why?" Ellen asked, leaning against the kitchen counter. "Is something wrong at home?"

"Tom says he thinks he found a buyer for the Montana house."

Tanya returned from the window. "Already? That was fast."

"I'm having second thoughts about selling it," Sue admitted. "I don't think I can give up Mo Mummy."

"You can do hard things," Ellen reminded her. "Think about what we just went through."

Sue shook her head. "You don't understand."

"It's a thrill," Tanya said, sitting at the table beside her. "Like what we get when we save souls, right?"

Sue nodded. "But I don't have to wait to feel that sensation two or three times a year. I can have it every day at the casino."

"Only when you win," Ellen argued.

"It's the possibility of winning that thrills me," Sue explained. "It gives me a reason to get out of bed each day. I want to go back."

"What would your mother say?" Tanya asked. "Would she approve?"

"She liked to gamble," Sue said defensively.

Ellen leaned forward. "Every day?"

"No. Not every day. Only when we went cruising together."

Tanya put an arm around their friend. "I wish I knew how to help you."

"Tom wants me to see a shrink."

"I think that's a good idea," Ellen agreed. "Please, Sue. You can't go on like this."

Sue stood up from her seat to refill her coffee. "Let's focus on these ghosts. How are we going to help them?"

Tanya straightened her back. "We could do a crossover ceremony *en masse*, like we did at the Hoover Dam and in Santa Fe."

Ellen sat across from Tanya at the table, holding the warm cup of coffee in both hands. "I don't know if that would work as well as it did in those places. We knew the descendants of the ghosts, and we—or the descendants—called the ghosts by name, remember? Here, we don't even know who we're dealing with—aside from Charles McElvaine."

"Then, let's start with him," Sue suggested. "Maybe he can help us."

<u>CHAPTER TWENTY-SIX</u>

Messages from the Living and the Dead

Ellen double-checked the equipment cases by the door while Sue zipped the last of their gear into a duffel bag.

They stepped out into the cool morning and found C.W. already waiting at the curb, leaning against his SUV with a Styrofoam cup in hand. He looked up and grinned as they approached.

"Morning, ladies. You all look like you've seen a ghost."

"Funny," Sue muttered. "Too soon."

"We're stopping at the hospital first," Tanya explained as they climbed in. "We want to check on John."

"Got it." C.W. gave a small nod, his jovial expression dimming with respect. "I'll wait outside."

The ride was quiet, the tension thick in the car. No one spoke as they passed blooming dogwoods and old, red-brick buildings. Canadian geese stood in pairs on the grassy median. Ellen stared out the window, her thoughts circling.

Inside the hospital, they stopped at the gift shop to pick out flowers. Tanya chose a cheerful arrangement of yellow daisies and purple irises in a powder blue pot. Sue paid for it while Ellen added a small handwritten note: *Thank you for believing in us.*

They found John's room on the second floor. His wife, Christine, whom they'd met the night before, sat in a chair beside his bed, her hand wrapped around his.

"Oh," she said, startled as the three women entered. "Hi."

Tanya stepped forward and handed her the flower arrangement. "We just wanted to check on him. And on you."

Christine's eyes filled with tears as she accepted the flowers. "Thank you. That's very kind." She looked back at her husband. "He's stable. No swelling in the brain. But he hasn't woken up."

Ellen approached the bed, her heart tight. John looked pale and still, his skin nearly the same color as the hospital sheet. Machines beeped quietly around him.

"We're so sorry," Ellen said.

Christine nodded, brushing hair from John's forehead. "I know you are. And I don't blame you." She looked down. "This wasn't your fault. You were trying to help John, the museum."

There was a pause before she glanced back up at them. "Have you heard about George Flint?"

Ellen exchanged a look with Sue and Tanya. "No," she said slowly. "What's happened?"

Christine's jaw tightened. "They found his body this morning, in the windmill tower."

Ellen gasped. "Oh, my God."

"No signs of trauma," Christine continued. "But no clear cause of death either. It's like he just . . . died."

Sue let out a long breath. "The portal."

"He chose to stay," Ellen explained. "We warned him."

"I can't pretend to begin to understand what you're talking about," Christine said with a shrug. "All I know is that I feel awful saying it, but I'm glad he's dead."

Ellen blinked before glancing at her friends.

Christine shook her head. "I shouldn't say that. I'm not that kind of person. But after what he did to John? I could have killed him myself."

Ellen reached out and touched her arm. "You're angry. You have every right to be."

Christine gave a shaky nod. "I'll let you know if there's any change."

"Please do," Tanya said. "We're heading to Greenfield Village next."

Christine looked up. "To the windmill?"

"No," Ellen replied. "Menlo Lab."

"We just need to tie up a few loose ends," Sue added.

They took their leave, walking back to the parking lot in a solemn line. The weight of Christine's words settled over them. If the portal had claimed George Flint, how close had they come to sharing his fate? Would they have been similarly discovered dead in the tower?

Ellen could only imagine how Brian and her children and grandchildren would have reacted had she decided, like George, to stay. Tears welled in her eyes and slipped down her cheeks. She wiped her face with the back of her hand as they exited the hospital.

C.W. sat behind the wheel of the white SUV, tapping on his phone, but looked up as they approached.

"Everything okay?" he asked as they climbed in.

"Not really," Ellen murmured, buckling her seatbelt. "George Flint is dead. They found him in the windmill."

C.W.'s brows shot up. "Whoa."

Tanya leaned forward. "Can you take us to Greenfield Village?"

"You bet."

During the ride, C.W. asked about George, and they filled him in on their theory about the portal—about George wanting to stay. The driver also asked about John, and the friends repeated what they'd been told—stable but still unconscious.

When he pulled up to the curb in front of Greenfield Village, C.W. asked, "Should I wait here? Or do you think it'll be a while?"

"Maybe we should text you when we're ready," Sue replied as she climbed out and headed toward the back of the SUV for their gear.

As C.W. opened the cargo door, Ellen said to C.W., "You don't have to be at our beck and call, you know. If you've got things to do, we can use the Uber app."

"I know," he said as he handed her a bag. "But I don't want to miss out on any exciting developments in your case."

"You're the best," Ellen said with a smile. She paid him for the ride, along with a generous tip. "Tanya will text you when we're ready."

As they approached Menlo Lab, Ellen noticed yellow crime-scene tape fluttering in the breeze around the Farris Windmill. Police cars and a coroner's van blocked the gravel path leading to the tower. Officers moved about with quiet urgency, taking photographs and measuring the scene.

"I didn't think they'd still be here," Tanya murmured. "Do you think George's body is still in there?"

"I don't know," Ellen replied, glancing at the coroner's van. "Probably."

Inside Menlo Lab, the air was thick with the scents of old wood and machine oil. They arranged their equipment: EMF detectors, voice recorders, the spirit box, and full-spectrum cameras. Sue lit a protective candle and set it on a high shelf.

Ellen placed the sketchbook with the image of Edison's device on the central table. "All right, Charles," she said aloud. "If you're still with us, we could use your help."

The EMF detector pulsed green.

Sue turned on the spirit box. The crackling static gave way to a few disjointed words: "Here . . . okay."

"Charles McElvaine?" Ellen asked. "Is that you?"

She listened to the pulsing static coming over the spirit box. After a moment, the word "Yes" came through, loud and clear.

"Do you know if the portal created by Thomas Edison is now closed?" Sue asked. "Was our mission a success?"

They waited. After another moment had passed, the word "yes" came through again.

Ellen felt a chill run up her spine. Paul had done it. He'd pulled the trigger.

Sue leaned forward. "Charles, we need the names of anyone who passed through to this side while the portal was open. Anyone who may be trapped here with us. Can you help?"

The static surged. "No."

The three friends exchanged looks of disappointment.

"Maybe he doesn't know who they are," Sue speculated beneath her breath.

"What do we do now?" Tanya whispered.

They were startled when another phrase came over the spirit box, "Hat . . . man."

"Is this Thomas Alva Edison?" Ellen asked, eyes wide.

A beat of silence. Then: "Charles."

Sue wrinkled her nose. "What about the Hat Man? What are you trying to tell us?"

"Stayed," the spirit box said.

"Stayed?" Ellen repeated. "Are you saying that Thomas Edison stayed behind?"

"Yes," the spirit box said.

"Where?" Sue asked. "Is he here with you?"

"No," the spirit box said.

"Maybe he's at the Eloise," Tanya whispered.

"Yes," the spirit box said.

"But why?" Ellen wondered aloud.

"Children," the voice replied.

Ellen exchanged a look with Sue and Tanya. "What children?"

No answer.

"Do you think he means the children we saw in the mirror?" Sue asked Ellen and Tanya.

"Is he trying to protect them?" Tanya whispered.

"But they were afraid of him, remember?" Sue said.

Ellen straightened. "We need to go back there."

Sue nodded slowly. "But what about you, Charles? Are you ready to move on?"

A brief pause. Then: "Yes."

Ellen stepped forward and lowered her voice. "Then let us help you. You've helped us more than we can say."

Sue and Tanya joined her, the three women holding hands in a tight circle.

"We call upon the loved ones of Charles McElvaine," Ellen said gently. "His parents, his wife—anyone who loved him in life. Come and guide him to peace. And we call upon God's heavenly angels and saints. Please open the doors of heaven and welcome Charles home."

"Surround him in light," Tanya added. "Show him the way."

"Let him feel your embrace," Sue whispered. "Let him know he's not alone."

At first, nothing happened. Ellen closed her eyes and prayed for the soul of Charles McElvaine. She opened them again when she heard a rattle. The electric chair! It had begun to tremble softly against the floorboards. A warm light gathered above it—dim at first, then growing brighter, swirling like a vortex of gold.

Ellen's heart pounded as the light engulfed the chair, then slowly faded.

The spirit box went silent. The candle flame flickered out.

The women stood frozen, tears in their eyes. The lab felt lighter, almost buoyant, as if a burden had finally lifted.

Sue wiped her cheek. "He made it."

"How do you know?" Ellen asked.

"I saw," Sue said with a broad smile, still wiping tears from her cheeks. "With my mind's eye, I saw him go."

CHAPTER TWENTY-SEVEN

Return to the Eloise

The bright afternoon sun filtered through a hazy sky as Ellen, Sue, and Tanya exited Menlo Lab with their equipment cases in hand. The air was heavy with springtime humidity as they made their way toward the Greenfield Village visitor lot.

True to his word, C.W. was waiting for them in his white SUV, the engine idling. He leaned out the window and waved as they approached.

"Any luck?" he called.

"Somewhat," Tanya stated as she climbed up front beside him.

C.W. lifted his brow. "Where to?"

"The Golden Fleece," Tanya said from the front passenger's seat. "We're craving gyros."

"Say no more."

As C.W. pulled onto the road, Ellen recalled the way the windmill had looked that morning, cordoned off with yellow tape and guarded by a few stoic officers. The image of George Flint lying lifeless inside the tower flickered in her mind like a faded slide.

"Anything new about Flint?" C.W. asked, glancing in the rearview mirror.

Ellen shook her head. "Only that it still doesn't make sense. His body was found, but no clear cause of death. He just . . . died."

"It's because he chose to stay on the other side," Sue reminded them. "It was his choice."

"We think Edison's ghost might still be active," Tanya said. "The ghost of Charles McElvaine—the kid that was executed by Edison's electric chair—told us to find him at the Eloise."

C.W. stopped at a red light. "I knew that place would be important to your case. Didn't I tell you?"

"We couldn't have done any of this without you," Sue admitted.

Ellen leaned forward. "Could you reach out to Shannon? See if she'd let us back in tonight?"

"I'll text her as soon as I drop you off," he promised.

They pulled up to the Golden Fleece and Ellen and her friends climbed out of the SUV, the smell of lamb and onions wafting through the open door. Ellen paid C.W. and thanked him again before following her friends to the restaurant. The small, cozy diner buzzed with energy: the sizzle of meat on the grill, the clink of silverware, and the chatter of locals enjoying a late lunch.

The women claimed a table near the window, placing their orders quickly—three gyros with fries and iced teas all around.

"So," Sue said, unwrapping her silverware, "why do you think Edison went back to the Eloise?"

Tanya folded her hands on the table. "What if he's experimenting again? We know he had ambitions about helping the living to communicate with the dead. Maybe he's using the asylum to try again."

"With those children's spirits?" Ellen asked. "Charles said 'children.' What if Edison's trying to protect them?"

Sue frowned. "Or use them. They were afraid of him, remember? They warned us to stay away from him."

The thought made Ellen's stomach twist.

"We need to go in prepared," Tanya said. "If Edison has unfinished business at the Eloise, it could be dangerous."

Ellen nodded. "We don't confront him unless we know why he stayed. And if he's still operating under Flint's influence—"

"Then we shut him down," Sue finished.

"How could that be possible?" Tanya argued. "We have the secret journal. Flint's gone."

"We just need to be prepared for anything," Ellen explained. "Even things that seem unlikely or improbable."

Their conversation paused as their server arrived with plates of steaming gyros and golden fries. Ellen took a long sip of her tea, then unwrapped her gyro, grateful for the distraction.

A moment later, Sue's phone buzzed. She wiped her hands and checked the screen.

"It's a text from Tom." Her voice wavered slightly, "The buyer made an offer. Above asking price."

Tanya looked up from her plate. "Already?"

"He wants to accept," Sue said, staring at the screen. "He's asking if I agree."

Ellen lowered her sandwich. "What do you think?"

Sue hesitated. "I don't know. Part of me wants to say yes. But the other part—the Mo Mummy part—wants one more trip."

Tanya smiled. "Then take it. We'll go with you to visit before closing."

"I agree," Ellen added. "You need closure, and so do we. That place was part of all our lives."

Sue looked down at her phone, thumbs hovering over the screen. She typed out her reply, pressed send, and let out a breath. "Well, that's that."

"You made the right call," Ellen said.

Sue picked at her fries. "It just feels . . . final, you know?"

"It is," Tanya said gently. "But it's not the end. Just a new chapter."

Tanya's phone buzzed. She picked up her phone and read the screen. "It's a text from C.W."

"What does it say?" Sue prompted.

Tanya read, "'Just heard back from Shannon. We're good for tonight. She'll meet us at 10 p.m.'"

"Then it's settled," Sue said. "Tonight, we return to the Eloise."

The moon floated high above the silhouette of the Eloise Asylum as C.W.'s white SUV pulled into the parking lot. It was ten o'clock sharp, and the night was silent except for the soft purr of the idling engine.

"You ladies sure about this?" C.W. asked, glancing back at them from the driver's seat.

"As sure as we can be," Ellen replied, adjusting the strap of her bag filled with her equipment.

C.W. nodded solemnly and reached for his phone. "Shannon said she'd meet you by the side entrance. She's already there."

The trio paid and thanked him and stepped out into the night air, bags in hand. Sue took the lead as they made their way to the metal door at the side of the building. Ellen had to admit that Sue's gambling addiction had put her in the best shape of her post-childbirth life.

Shannon was there waiting for them, arms crossed, flashlight in hand. Her ponytail swung as she turned to greet them.

"I thought y'all had had enough of this place," she said, unlocking the door.

"We thought so, too," Sue muttered.

"Standard procedure," Shannon said, handing them each a clipboard with a waiver attached. "Sign again. Just in case."

They signed in silence, the soft scratching of pens the only sound before Shannon handed them a key.

"Same as before. Lock the door behind you when you go in and when you come out. Put the key in the drop box." With a nod and a nervous smile, she turned and disappeared into the darkness.

Ellen shut the door behind them and locked it. The thick silence of the building enveloped them immediately.

They wasted no time. Climbing to the third floor, they moved with purpose to the hydrotherapy room. Ellen remembered the shiver she'd felt here before—when the children had appeared in the mirror's reflection.

"I hate how quiet it is," Tanya whispered, peering down the long hallway.

"It's never quiet here," Ellen said. "It just pretends to be."

Inside the hydrotherapy room, the mirror loomed large and foreboding. They placed their equipment on the floor and began setting up: EMF detector, full-spectrum cameras, electromagnetic generator, and the spirit box. Their headlights flickered faintly, illuminating the cracked tiles.

Sue powered on the spirit box. Static filled the room, followed by the faint stutter of shifting frequencies. Tanya adjusted the microphone on her EVP recorder.

"Is anyone here with us?" Ellen asked gently. "Are the children we saw before still with us?"

The box crackled. Then: "Patricia."

Ellen's breath caught. "Patricia, how old are you?"

After a long pause, the word "ten" came over the box.

"That's what she said last time," Tanya whispered. "It might be the same ghost."

"Are there others with you?" Sue asked.

Nearly a full minute passed before another word came over the box:

"Yes."

"How many?" Ellen asked.

This time the reply came more quickly: "Four."

Sue stepped toward the mirror, where the only reflections that greeted them were their own. "Are you safe?"

The spirit box crackled for over a minute. Ellen worried that Charles McElvaine had given them bad information. Maybe the Hat Man wasn't here after all. Maybe none of the spirits here were willing to communicate with them.

"Are you in danger?" Ellen finally asked. "Are we in danger?"

Again, a minute passed with no response. Tanya sighed in the quiet.

"Patricia?" Sue asked. "Are you still here with us?"

Nothing.

"Maybe we scared them away," Tanya whispered.

"Maybe we're in the wrong place," Sue said. "Let's try the second floor, where we saw the Hat Man."

They packed up quickly and descended to the second floor, making their way to the corridor where they'd twice encountered the silhouette. The air felt thicker here, heavier, charged.

"Let's do the Estes Method," Tanya suggested. "I'll go under."

Ellen and Sue exchanged a look but nodded. Tanya was the most intuitive, the most open. If anyone could connect, it was her.

"I need to be able to sway and put myself into a trance," Tanya said. "I guess I could sit on the floor."

"How about that dentist's chair?" Sue suggested.

"That's too creepy," Tanya said with a shudder.

"Creepier than this dirty floor?" Ellen challenged.

"Good point."

Tanya sat on the dusty dentist's chair, slipping on the blindfold and noise-canceling headphones. Ellen plugged the headphones into the spirit box so that only Tanya would be able to hear what came over it.

Ellen and Sue stood a few feet away from Tanya with their headlights on.

"Spirits of the other realm," Sue began, "we come in peace. We mean you no harm."

Sue quickly introduced them by name to any spirits that might be present.

"Calling Thomas Alva Edison," Ellen said. "Are you here with us? Please give us a sign."

Sue's headlamp flickered.

Tanya spoke: "Hello, hello, hello."

Sue raised her eyebrows. "That's him. That has to be him."

"Is that you, Thomas Alva Edison?" Ellen asked. "Please give us confirmation if it is."

"Okay," Tanya said. "Yes. It's me."

Sue's eyes widened. "Thank you for that."

Ellen continued. "Why are you still here? The portal is closed."

Tanya tilted her head. "Work. Not done."

"What kind of work?" Sue asked.

"Light," Tanya said.

Ellen exchanged puzzled glances with Sue.

"The light bulb?" Ellen wondered aloud.

"Energy," Tanya said. Then she added, "Guide."

"Can you tell us more?" Sue asked.

"Guide," Tanya said again.

"Guide who?" Ellen asked.

"Children," Tanya said.

"Where are you guiding the children to?" Sue asked with a look of concern on her face.

"Other realm," Tanya said.

"Oh!" Ellen snapped her fingers. "I see now."

"You're trying to help the children cross over?" Sue asked with a look of surprise.

"Yes . . . and others."

Before Ellen or Sue could ask more, Tanya added, "Lost. Afraid. So many."

"How are you able to help them?" Ellen asked.

"New invention," Tanya said.

In the doorway, a pinpoint of light appeared.

Ellen gasped. "Is that you? That light?"

"New invention," Tanya said again. Then, "I'm going now."

"Where?" Sue asked. "Where are you going?"

Tanya cleared her throat. "Third."

Ellen and Sue glanced at one another anxiously.

"The third floor?" Ellen wondered.

"Let's go up there," Sue said eagerly. "Hurry."

Ellen touched Tanya's shoulder. "That's good."

Tanya pulled off the blindfold and headphones, blinking. "Did any of that make sense?"

"Follow us upstairs, and we'll explain on the way," Ellen said.

As they rushed down the hall and up the stairs, Sue quickly relayed what they'd learned. Edison wasn't tormenting the children. He was trying to help them. He was building something, a light-based invention, to help lost souls find their way.

They reached the hydrotherapy room. After they entered, Ellen glanced back at the door to see the familiar silhouette of the Hat Man, just standing there.

A chill crept up her spine.

Sue's voice was a whisper. "Turn off your lights. Let's use the mirror."

One by one, they switched off their headlamps. The room plunged into darkness, broken only by the soft glow of their infrared camera's screen. Ellen turned it toward the mirror.

There they were. Five children. Barely visible to the naked eye, but clear. They stood silently looking back at them.

Ellen shivered and again glanced behind her, seeing no one.

Then—

A pinprick of light bloomed beside the Hat Man. Small. Gentle. Pulsing like a heartbeat.

The children turned to look.

"Follow the light," Ellen encouraged them. "It's safe."

One of the girls shook her head. Her translucent form trembled.

Sue's voice broke the silence. "I don't blame her. I'm not sure I trust him either."

The Hat Man did something none of them expected. He stepped fully into the room, visible not just in the mirror but before them, no longer a shadow. The brim of his hat tilted slightly as he reached into his coat pocket and pulled out a toy. A worn, stuffed lamb.

Patricia gasped. "That was mine."

Edison—no longer the Hat Man, but the ghost of a man trying to make amends—held the toy out to her. The child stepped forward, and the others followed.

Together, they walked toward the light.

And vanished.

A hush settled over the room.

"I saw it," Sue whispered, eyes brimming. "With my mind's eye. They crossed."

The shadow returned one last time. This time, not foreboding, but grateful. He tipped his hat.

And then he, too, was gone.

The children of the Eloise were at peace.

The streetlights of Dearborn flickered past in streaks of amber and gold as C.W.'s white SUV hummed along the dark road. The air inside was filled with the scent of coffee from cups C.W. had brought them earlier, now mostly empty, resting in cupholders.

Ellen sat in the back seat, head tilted slightly against the window. The coolness of the glass soothed her temple, but her mind buzzed with all they had witnessed.

"I still can't believe what we saw," Sue said quietly beside her.

"Me neither," Tanya murmured from the front passenger's seat. "Five children, now finally at peace, thanks to Thomas Edison."

"I have to admit," Ellen said, rubbing her temples, "I didn't expect Edison to earn my trust. Not after everything. But that—what he did—was real. That was redemption."

C.W. glanced at Ellen in the rearview mirror. "You don't think he's evil anymore?"

"No," Ellen said. "He's not just trying to atone. He's actively helping souls find their way."

Sue leaned forward. "You know what gets me? The toy. That lamb. He remembered her. Or he reached across dimensions and found it for her. Either way—it meant something."

Tanya sighed, leaning her head against the window. "So now what?"

There was a pause, filled only by the hum of the tires and the occasional click of C.W.'s turn signal.

Then, Tanya bolted upright. "Wait. I know what to do!"

Ellen leaned forward, brows furrowed. "Well, spill the beans!"

"The ghosts in Greenfield Village," Tanya said. "The ones who came through when the portal was open. Maybe Edison and his new invention can help them, like he helped the children at the Eloise."

Ellen sat up straighter. "That's a great idea, Tanya. He's the one who opened the portal. He should be the one to guide those souls home."

Sue lifted a finger beside Ellen. "Why don't we use the phonograph at Menlo Lab to call him to Greenfield Village?"

"Another great idea," Ellen said, happy now that they had a plan to help the rest of the lost souls.

C.W. grinned. "You three are something else. Running back to haunted buildings like you're inviting ghosts for brunch."

Ellen smiled. "It's what we do."

"Just promise me you'll be careful," he said, pulling into the drive of the Patrick Henry House. "I like being your driver, not your emergency contact."

The SUV came to a stop beneath the soft glow of the porch light. The historic colonial home stood quiet and still, its windows dark, the hour late.

Tanya reached for the door handle. "Thanks again, C.W."

They paid and said goodnight with promises to text him in the morning. Then they made their way inside the Patrick Henry House. As the door closed behind them, Ellen felt the weariness seep into her bones—but beneath it, a flicker of hope.

They had a plan. And tomorrow, they'd return to Menlo Lab to set it in motion.

<u>CHAPTER TWENTY-EIGHT</u>

Final Request

The hallway outside John Coleman's hospital room on Friday morning smelled of lemon-scented cleaner and antiseptic. Christine had called Ellen while she and her friends were having breakfast at the Patrick Henry House to say that John was awake, but she hadn't said anything more. Tanya had immediately texted C.W. for a ride, and now Ellen and her friends stood just outside the doorway of John's room, unsure for a beat if they should enter.

Christine Coleman sat beside her husband's bed, her hand wrapped gently around his. Her head was bowed in quiet reverence or exhaustion or maybe both. Then, as if sensing them, she looked up. Her face brightened with relief.

"You're here," she whispered, rising quickly and opening the door wider. "Come in, please. He's been asking for you."

Ellen stepped forward first, heart thudding, eyes immediately finding John's face. His color was better—still pale, but no longer the ashen gray of the day before. His eyes were open, tired but focused, and when he saw the three women approaching, a smile tugged at the corners of his lips.

"Well," he said, voice hoarse, "looks like I missed quite the adventure."

Sue laughed softly, brushing a tear from her cheek. "You scared the heck out of us, John."

"I scared myself," he murmured, then glanced at Christine. "But someone made sure I wasn't alone."

Ellen pushed her hair behind her ear. "We're so glad you're back."

"I heard something, while I was out," he said slowly. "Faint whispers, like wind through tall grass. I thought maybe I'd crossed over."

"You almost did," Tanya said gently. "You were out cold when we found you at the gate."

John blinked and smiled widely. "The things I do for that museum."

"No kidding," Christine said with a laugh.

"But it must have worked," John added. "I called to check on my staff this morning and was told that the windmill is no longer whispering. I owe you ladies a debt of gratitude, and more. Mission accomplished, it seems."

Christine gave a sharp nod. "It's true. One of his docents said it felt like the Village took a deep breath and finally exhaled."

John let out a long, slow breath himself, eyes glistening. "Thank God."

"There's more," Sue said, pulling a chair closer to his bedside. "Edison seems to have stayed behind."

John's eyes widened. "Edison's ghost?"

Ellen leaned forward. "He said there was more work to be done. He's not trapped. He chose to remain. He's invented a device that helps lost souls to find their way. We saw him help five child spirits at the Eloise cross over last night."

"A new device from beyond the grave?" John raised his brow. "That's astonishing. What about the necrophone?"

Tanya shrugged. "It's the same concept as the EVP recorder. I guess technology has advanced and surpassed it."

John clicked his tongue. "I still can't believe that George Flint was capable of what he did—blackmailing Edison, assaulting me."

Christine's hand flew to her mouth. "Oh, yeah. I haven't told him yet."

John's expression darkened. "Told me what?"

"George Flint," Christine began, glancing at Ellen at then back at John. "He's dead. His body was found in the windmill the morning after he attacked you." She looked away. "I shouldn't say this, but I'm glad he's gone. After what he did to you—"

Ellen gently touched Christine's shoulder. "We understand."

John was quiet for a moment, then asked, "Is it over, then?"

"Not quite," Ellen said. "There's one more thing we need to do."

Tanya straightened. "We think there are still souls wandering Greenfield Village—ghosts that came through the portal but never made it back."

"We want to call on Edison again," Sue explained. "Ask him to use his new invention—the one that helped those children at the Eloise cross over—to do the same for the lost spirits still out there."

"We're going back to Menlo Lab," Ellen said. "We're going to call him through the phonograph."

John blinked, clearly moved. "You're remarkable, all three of you. If there's anything I can do—"

"You've done enough," Tanya said with a gentle smile. "You've survived. And we're so grateful."

Christine placed a hand on John's shoulder and turned to Ellen. "We'll call if anything changes."

Ellen nodded. "And if you need anything—anything at all—you know how to reach us."

They said their goodbyes and left the room, stepping out into the cool, sterile light of the hospital corridor.

Ellen looked at her friends and took a deep breath. "I can't wait to see the back of this case."

"One last mission," Sue said with a reassuring smile.

Tanya's eyes glinted with resolve. "To Menlo Lab."

The clouds rolled in as C.W.'s SUV pulled up to the gate of Greenfield Village. Ellen glanced at the brick paths and quaint rooftops beyond. The air held a breathless stillness, as if the whole park were waiting.

"You want me to wait?" C.W. asked, his hand still on the gearshift. "Or do you want to text me when you're ready?"

Ellen looked over her shoulder at him as she climbed from the vehicle. "We'll text you."

He gave her a long look, then reached over to pop the back door. "Then go do what you do best."

They thanked him and retrieved their gear before heading toward Menlo Lab.

The familiar creak of the door greeted them as they stepped inside, the air dry and still, like a breath held too long. Dust particles danced in the shafts of the afternoon light, and the room smelled faintly of varnished wood and machine oil.

Ellen flicked on the overhead lights and crossed to the phonograph. It stood exactly where they'd left it, its horn gleaming with a dull, golden sheen. She ran her hand along its edge, whispering, "We're back, Mr. Edison."

She helped Sue and Tanya set up the equipment quickly and with practiced ease, though a silence hung over the trio. Not fear exactly—but gravity.

"What if he doesn't come?" Tanya asked, glancing toward the window.

"He will," Ellen said. "He has to. This is *his* unfinished business."

Sue adjusted the spirit box and set it beside the phonograph. "Okay. Let's warm it up."

A low, rhythmic crackle filled the room as the device powered on, static humming beneath their feet. Tanya struck a match and lit a white pillar candle, placing it beside the phonograph.

Ellen held an EMF detector in one hand and SLS camera in another. "Thomas Alva Edison," she said, her voice steady, "we ask for your presence. There are still souls here who need your help."

Nothing.

Ellen bit her lip. This had to work. They couldn't leave until it did.

"Please answer us," Sue urged. "You opened the portal. You need to help the souls who are trapped here in Greenfield Village. Use your device to help them find the other side."

A click. The phonograph needle jerked slightly. The horn hissed with a burst of static—and then silence.

Tanya frowned. "Try again."

Ellen took a breath. "Tom, Al, Thomas Alva Edison, the device you built helped five children at the Eloise Asylum find peace. There are more who need you now. Please. We need you to show them the way."

The phonograph clicked again. A faint hum—mechanical and musical—rose from its horn.

Then, slowly, a man's voice, distorted but unmistakable, emerged. "Hello, hello, hello."

"Thank goodness," Tanya murmured.

Ellen swallowed hard. "Is it really you, Thomas Edison?"

"Yes."

The word was quieter, almost weary, but filled with unmistakable warmth.

Sue straightened beside the phonograph. "We think there are still ghosts wandering the Village—souls who slipped through the portal before it closed. Will you help them?"

There was a pause, then a low, vibrating hum that wasn't quite sound—a presence, thick and electric, filled the air.

"They must be gathered."

Sue leaned in. "Can you do that?"

"No. You must."

Ellen frowned. "How? We don't even know how many there are—or who."

"Crank the music," Edison's voice instructed. "The phonograph will draw them here."

Sue glanced at Ellen and Tanya before she took the handle and cranked the phonograph.

The machine clicked again, then began to play something entirely new. It wasn't a recording they'd heard before—delicate harmonic pulses layered with soft static, rhythmic and pulsing like a heartbeat. Light shimmered faintly at the corners of the room as an old-fashioned melody played.

Then, the temperature dropped.

Ellen turned slowly, goosebumps rising along her arms. Through the frosted glass of the lab's side windows, faint silhouettes began to appear. Men and women in outdated clothing. Children with curious eyes. Workers in overalls. Women in long dresses. Dozens of them.

Ghosts.

Ellen gasped, heart pounding. "It's working. Keep cranking, Sue!"

The music came over the machine more clearly now, and the lab became even colder than the temperature outside. Ellen could feel the arrival of multiple spirits before she saw them. She wasn't sure if she saw them with her mind's eye or her literal eyes, but they were there, crowding into the room, surrounding the phonograph. The hair on the back of Ellen's neck stood on end. Her heart seemed to stop in her chest, and she could no longer tell if she was breathing.

Tanya stood beside her, trembling. "There's so many of them—more than I thought."

Somehow, Sue continued to crank the phonograph.

Then, near the doorway, the silhouette of the Hat Man appeared: Thomas Alva Edison. His image shifted and shimmered until Ellen could see him clear as day.

"Do you see him?" she whispered to her friends.

In her peripheral vision, she saw them nod.

Then, a pinpoint of light, like the one they saw at the Eloise, appeared beside him, near his hand. Ellen could just make out a device that resembled a tire pressure gauge.

The EMF detector in Ellen's hand was blinking red, but Ellen's eyes could not be pulled from the vision of Thomas Edison and his device.

A narrow cone of bluish-white light shone from its center, sweeping slowly through the room. The beam struck one of the figures—and the ghost glowed, faintly at first, then brighter, as if lit from within. Others followed.

And one by one, the ghosts began to fade.

Some smiled. Some waved. Some simply closed their eyes and let go.

A little girl in a pinafore looked directly at Ellen. Her lips moved—thank you. Then she vanished into the light.

Tanya gasped. "Did you see that?"

Ellen, unable to speak, nodded.

The light in the lab grew warmer. Brighter. The air shimmered with energy.

Then, just as quickly as it began, it was over.

The light vanished. The Hat Man faded, and Ellen and her friends were alone in the room.

Sue stopped cranking the phonograph and stood beside Ellen, catching her breath.

Ellen blinked and looked at her friends.

The only sound was the soft buzz of the overhead light.

Ellen turned to Sue. "Is it done?"

Sue looked around, stunned. "I think so. I saw them cross over. I think they're at peace."

Tanya brushed a tear from her cheek. "That felt like grace."

They stood in silence for a moment, the weight of everything they'd witnessed settling gently on their shoulders.

Then the phonograph crackled one last time, moving entirely on its own.

"Thank you. Remember me not by my errors, but by the light."

Ellen sucked in her lips. Then, she stepped forward and rested her fingers on the horn. "We will, Mr. Edison! We promise!"

After a beat, they packed their gear in reverent silence. As they stepped outside, the sun broke through the clouds and bathed Greenfield Village in soft, golden light.

No whispers. No shadows.

Just peace.

"C.W. is ten minutes away," Tanya said, breaking the silence. "And I'm starving."

"You and me both, sister," Sue said. "I could eat a horse."

"I want gyros again," Ellen admitted. "I can't seem to get enough of those."

"I was thinking the very same thing," Sue confessed.

"The Golden Fleece?" Tanya asked as she followed them to the curb to wait for their ride.

"Yes, please!" Ellen cried.

CHAPTER TWENTY-NINE

Return to Talks to Buffalo Lodge

The sky over Montana stretched wide and wild, streaked with lavender clouds as the sun began its slow descent behind the pine-covered hills as Ellen and her friends pulled into the circular drive at *Talks to Buffalo Lodge*. The log-and-stone house stood stoic, golden in the last light, its porch draped in shadows and old memories.

Sue was quiet in the back seat. Her eyes, glassy with unspoken emotion, remained fixed on the front door.

"You okay?" Tanya asked gently from the front passenger's seat.

Sue didn't answer at first. Then she gave a small, tight nod. "I think so."

Ellen reached over and touched her friend's hand. "We've got time. Say goodbye the way you need to."

They stepped out into the crisp, pine-scented air. A chill lingered in the breeze. Unlike in San Antonio—and even in Detroit—springtime did not look as though it had arrived. The three women stood for a moment, staring up at the house. It looked exactly the same—and yet nothing was the same.

Sue inhaled deeply. "Let's go in."

Inside, the air held a faint scent of cedar and old stone. Everything looked exactly as Ellen had last seen it: cathedral ceilings in the living area with exposed wooden beams, a stone fireplace, and resting on the mantel was Ellen's painting of the white buffalo as it had appeared to her during their investigation of the ghost of Blackfeet Nation. And in front of the hearth was the original wooden bench that once held the sacred hide.

Sue moved slowly through the entryway, her fingers trailing across the back of the leather couch, then along the white, granite countertop, its silver veins bringing out the gray in the painted kitchen cabinets. Ellen still loved their design and was sad that she would never cook in that kitchen again.

Sue didn't say much as she made her way from room to room—just silent, slow movements, the kind of wordless farewell that didn't need explaining. Ellen and Tanya followed behind, both upstairs and down, giving her space, saying nothing.

They eventually gathered in the living room, where Sue stood before the stone fireplace. The poker set was still neatly arranged. A few logs were stacked to the side. It would've been so easy to light a fire, brew some tea, and fall into the old rhythm of their Montana retreats. Ellen felt the pull of that nostalgia—how many evenings had they spent here, talking ghosts and grandchildren, sipping wine or hot cocoa after a day visiting Glacier National Park?

"I thought I needed one more night here," Sue finally said. Her voice was low but steady. "But I don't."

Tanya sat on the edge of the armchair. "You sure?"

Sue nodded. "This place holds a lot of memories, but none of them will disappear just because I let go of the property."

Ellen stepped beside her. "You're keeping the best parts of it—us, the memories, the meaning."

Sue laughed softly. "Yeah. And the grandkids didn't like coming here anyway. After last Christmas, Lexi and Stephen said never again. The flight was too much for them."

"I can understand that," Tanya put in.

"They're still too young to appreciate this place, anyway," Ellen added.

"I suppose you're right," Sue agreed.

Ellen watched her closely. "How do you feel?"

Sue breathed out slowly. "Sad. I really want to go to the casino one more time. Come with?"

They stepped outside onto the porch. The sun had dipped behind the trees, leaving a trail of orange and rose-tinted clouds overhead. A hawk circled in the distance. Somewhere nearby, an owl called softly.

"I want to say something to you, Sue," Tanya said suddenly.

Sue put her hands on her hips, in warrior-ready fashion. "I'm listening."

"There are others who need to win the grand, not you. I know it's exciting, but you have everything you need, and so many people don't. I'm not saying that poor people should play the slots, but what I am saying is that instead of begging the universe to let you hit the jackpot, let someone else have it."

Sue seemed to consider Tanya's words. "I hadn't really thought of it that way."

"You have a generous spirit, Sue," Ellen added. "I think you can follow Tanya's advice. You just need to find something else that can excite you on a regular basis—beyond the few trips we take together each year."

"I must admit that the research I've conducted so far on that Branson property has me entranced," Sue said. "It would be fun to start a new project, especially one surrounded by legends."

"Yes, it would," Tanya agreed.

They stood there in silence until Sue turned, one last time, and looked at the house. "Thank you," she whispered—not to them, but to the place itself.

They loaded into their rental, and as Ellen buckled her seatbelt behind the wheel, she glanced at Sue. "I'm proud of you."

"I'm proud of me too," Sue said with a nod. "No casino for me. I never thought I'd hear myself say that."

They were twenty miles down the road when Ellen broke the companionable silence. "So, tell us more about Branson."

Sue smiled but didn't look away from the window beside her. "Tom's already reached out to the listing agent. We'll hear back next week."

Tanya perked up. "Still thinking it's the perfect next chapter?"

"Property needs a lot of work," Sue said. "But it's big, secluded, and full of personality. I think it could be a great new headquarters."

"You mentioned legends?" Ellen asked.

Sue's grin widened. "According to a website I found, the estate includes a network of caves the Osage once called *Haunted Breath*. But somewhere in the last century, they picked up the name *Murder Caves*."

Tanya gave a delighted groan. "That sounds like our kind of place."

Sue nodded. "And there's more. Locals say a Confederate soldier-turned-bandit buried treasure in the caves after the war and never returned for it. Some think it's cursed. Others think it's guarded by the spirits of those he betrayed."

Ellen exchanged a look with Tanya. "So, we're talking hauntings and hidden treasure?"

"And possibly murder," Sue added, a twinkle in her eye.

Ellen laughed. "Sounds like the perfect location for Ghost Healers, Inc."

Sue's voice softened. "Maybe we name the new place *Talks to Spirits Lodge.*"

Tanya smiled. "Let's just make sure we don't *become* the spirits."

They all laughed as the road wound ahead of them, stretching into the dark.

***

THE END

Thank you for reading my story. I hope you enjoyed it! If you did, please consider leaving a review. Reviews help other readers to discover my books, which helps me.

Please visit my website at evapohler.com to get the next book, *A Sprite Christmas.*

Here's the blurb:

This holiday spirit doesn't want peace on Earth—just his gold.

When Sue convinces her husband to purchase a historic estate outside Branson, Missouri—rumored to hide a cache of lost gold—she ropes Ellen and Tanya into helping renovate the sprawling homestead over the Christmas holidays. But it doesn't take long for the trio to realize the real estate agent left out some key details . . . like the ghostly mischief plaguing the property.

What starts as harmless holiday chaos soon turns dark. The sprite haunting the estate isn't just mischievous—he's menacing. And his message is clear: the treasure stays buried, and trespassers won't be tolerated.

With Christmas looming and the hauntings escalating, Ellen, Tanya, and Sue must uncover the truth behind the legend before the spirit's antics turn deadly. Is this mystery house a festive fixer-upper—or a trap best left untouched?

EVA POHLER

Eva Pohler is a *USA Today* bestselling author of over thirty novels in multiple genres, including mysteries, thrillers, and young adult paranormal romance based on Greek mythology. Her books have been described as "addictive" and "sure to thrill"—*Kirkus Reviews*.

To learn more about Eva and her books, and to sign up to hear about new releases, and sales, please visit her website at https://www.evapohler.com.

Acknowledgments

I would like to thank the following premium members for their continued support:

Susan Albright

Amie Boutte

Lori Brooks

Debi Canon

Theresa Christ

Rebekka and Sherry Colegrove

Betty Downs

Amanda Ecker

Kerry Erickson

Laura Gimbel

Venette Grisham

Samie Hall-Rood

Shellie Hedge

Michelle Holloway

Misty Killion

Anita Klaboe

Leslie Lawrence

Carrie McCauley

Melissa Millar

Patrick Mitchell

Glorianna Murry

Rachel Renzo

Patricia Hand Salinas

Candy Smith

Debi Vap
Tammy Wojcik
Kristi Yates

9 781958 390832